CRYPT-CITY OF
THE DEATHLESS ONE

CRYPT-CITY OF
THE DEATHLESS ONE

HENRY KUTTNER

WILDSIDE PRESS

INTRODUCTION: HENRY KUTTNER

Henry Kuttner (1915–1958) was an American author of science fiction, fantasy, and horror. He was born in Los Angeles, California His father, a bookseller also named Henry Kuttner (1863–1920), had come from Prussia and lived in San Francisco since 1859; his mother, Annie Levy (1875–1954), came from Great Britain.

Henry grew up in relative poverty following the death of his father. As a young man, he worked in his spare time for the literary agency of his "uncle," Laurence D'Orsay (actually, his first cousin per marriage), in Los Angeles before selling his first story, "The Graveyard Rats," to *Weird Tales* in early 1936. It was while working for the d'Orsay agency that Kuttner picked Leigh Brackett's early manuscripts off the slush pile; it was under his tutelage that she sold her first story to John W. Campbell at *Astounding Stories*.

He was known for his literary prose and worked in close collaboration with his wife, C.L. Moore. They met through the "Lovecraft Circle," a group of writers and fans who corresponded with H. P. Lovecraft. Their work together spanned the 1940s and 1950s, and most of the work was credited to pseudonyms, mainly Lewis Padgett and Lawrence O'Donnell.

L. Sprague de Camp, who knew Kuttner and Moore well, has stated that their collaborations were so seamless that, after a story was completed, it was often impossible for either Kuttner or Moore to recall who had written what. According to de Camp, it was typical for either partner to break off from a story in mid-paragraph or even mid-sentence, with the latest page of the manuscript still in the typewriter. The other spouse would routinely continue the story where the first had left off. They alternated in this manner as many times as necessary until the story was finished.

Among his most popular work were the Gallegher stories, published under the Padgett name, about a man who invented high-tech solutions to client problems (assisted by his insufferably egomaniacal robot) when he was stinking drunk, only to be completely unable to remember exactly what he had built or why after sobering up. These stories were later collected in *Robots Have No Tails*. In her introduction to the 1973 Lancer Books edition, Moore stated that Kuttner wrote all the Gallegher stories himself.

Marion Zimmer Bradley is among many authors who have cited Kuttner as an influence. Her novel *The Bloody Sun* is dedicated to him. Roger Zelazny has talked about the influence of *The Dark World* on his Amber series.

Henry Kuttner's friend Richard Matheson dedicated his 1954 novel *I Am Legend* to Kuttner, with thanks for his help and encouragement. Ray Bradbury has said that Kuttner actually wrote the last 300 words of Bradbury's first horror story, "The Candle" (*Weird Tales*, November 1942).

Author Mary Elizabeth Counselman believed that Kuttner's habit of writing under widely varied pseudonyms deprived him of the fame that should have been his: "I have often wondered why Kuttner chose to hide his talents behind so many false faces for no editorial reason... Admittedly, the fun is in pretending to be someone else. But Kuttner cheated himself of much fame that he richly deserved by hiding his light under a bushel of pen names that many fans did not know were his. Seabury Quinn and I both chided him about this."

Henry Kuttner spent the middle 1950s getting his master's degree before dying of a heart attack in Los Angeles in 1958. With his passing, the field lost a master at far too young an age.

—Karl Wurf
Rockville, MD

CRYPT-CITY OF THE DEATHLESS ONE

CHAPTER I

Icy water splashed into Ed Garth's face and dripped down his tattered, grimy shirt. It was a tremendous effort to open his eyes. Fumes of the native Ganymedean rotgut liquor were swimming in his brain.

Someone was shaking him roughly. Garth's stocky body jerked convulsively. He struck out, his drink-swollen face twisted with frightened fury, and gasped, "*Ylgana! Vo m'trana al-khron—*"

The hand on his shoulder fell away. Someone said, "That's it, Paula! The Ancient Tongue!"

And a girl's voice, doubtful, a little disgusted.

"You're sure? But how in the System did this—this—"

"Bum. Tramp," Garth muttered, peering blearily at the pale ovals of unfocused faces above him. "Don't mind me, sister. Beachcomber is the word—drunk, right now. So please get the hell out and let me finish my bottle."

More water was sluiced on Garth. He shook his head, groaning, and saw Tolomo, the Ganymedean trader, scowling down at him. The native's three-pupiled eyes were angry.

English hissed, oddly accented, on his tongue.

"You wake up, Garth! Hear me? This is a job for you. You owe me too much already. These people come looking for you, say they want a guide. Now you do what they want, and pay me for all that liquor you buy on credit."

"Sure," Garth said wearily. "Tomorrow. Not now."

Tolomo snorted. "I get you native guides, Captain Brown. They know way to Chahnn."

The man's voice said stubbornly, "I don't want natives. I want Ed Garth."

"Well, you won't get him," Garth growled, pillowing his head on his arms. "This joint smells already, but you make it worse. Beat it."

He did not see Captain Brown slip Tolomo a folded credit-current. The trader deftly pocketed the money, nodded, and gripped Garth by the hair, lifting his head. The bluish, inhuman face was thrust into the Earthman's.

"Listen to me, Garth," Tolomo said, fairly spitting the words. "I let you come in here and get drunk all the time on the cuff. You pay me a little, not much, whenever you gather enough alka-roots to sell. But you owe plenty. People ask me why I let a bum like you come to my *Moonflower-Ritz Bar*—"

"That's a laugh," Garth mouthed. "A ramshackle plastic flophouse full of cockroaches and bad liquor. *Moonflower-Ritz*, hogwash!"

"Shut up," Tolomo snapped. "I let you run up a bill here when nobody else would. Now you take this job and pay me or I have the marshal put you in jail. At hard labor, in the swamps."

Garth called Tolomo something unprintable. "Okay," he groaned. "You win, louse. You know damn well no Earthman can stand swampwork, even with bog-shoes. Now let go of my hair before I smash your teeth in."

"You do it? You guide these people?"

"I said I would, didn't I?" Garth reached fumblingly for the bottle before him. Someone thrust a filled glass into his hand. He gulped the fiery purplish liquor, shuddered, and blew out his breath.

"Okay," he said. "Welcome to Ganymede, the pleasure spot of the System. The worst climate outside Hell, the only world almost completely unexplored, and the nicest place for going to the dogs I've ever seen. The Chamber of Commerce greets you. Here's the representative." He pointed to a six-legged lizard with the face of a gargoyle that scuttled over the table and leaped into the shadows where the light of the radio-lamp did not reach.

Captain Brown said, "I can offer you fifty dollars to guide us to the ruined city—Chahnn. And, maybe, I can offer you *ten thousand bucks* to do another little job for us."

* * * *

The shock of that was more effective than cold water had been. Garth jerked back, for the first time looking at his companions. There were two of them—a man and a girl, their neat tropical outfits looking out of a place in this grimy dive. The man was thin and bronzed, looking as though all the moisture had been boiled out of him by hot suns. He was made of tough leather, Garth thought. His face was the most expressionless one Garth had ever seen—pale, shallow eyes, a rat-trap mouth, and the general air of a tiger taking it easy.

The girl ... sudden sick pain struck through Garth. She looked like Moira. For an incredible moment he thought, with his liquor-dulled mind, that she had come back. But Moira was dead—had been, for nearly five years now.

Five years of living death—hitting the skids on Ganymede, where men go down fast. Garth's ravaged face hardened. He forced himself to look squarely at the girl.

She wasn't Moira, after all. She had the same look of sleek, clean femininity, but her hair was golden-red instead of brown, and her eyes were greenish, not blue. The softness in her face was belied by the stubborn, rounded chin.

"Ten thousand?" Garth repeated softly. "I don't get the picture. Any native could take you to Chahnn."

The girl said, "We know that. We're interested in—something else. Could you use ten grand?"

"Yeah! Yeah, I could," Garth said.

"What would you do with it? Go back to Earth? We might swing it so you could get a job there. There's been a shortage of men ever since the Silver Plague started."

Garth laid his fingers gently around the glass and squeezed, till the transparent plastic was bent out of shape. He didn't look at the girl.

"I'm through with Earth. If I could collect—ten thousand?—I'd commit suicide, in a very funny way. I'd go into the Black Forest. The money could get me the men and equipment I'd need, but—well, nobody gets out of the Black Forest alive."

"You did," Captain Brown said.

"Eh? You heard about that?"

"We've heard stories—plenty of them. About how you came out of the Black Forest six years ago, raving with fever and talking in a language nobody could understand. And how you've been taking trips into the Forest ever since. Just what happened? I know you tried to get up expeditions to rescue a man named Willard—he was with you, wasn't he?"

Garth felt again that sick deadness in his brain—the monstrous question that had been tormenting him for five years now. Abruptly he slammed his fist on the table. Tolomo's face appeared behind a curtain and vanished again as Brown waved him back.

"Forget it," Garth said. "Even on Ganymede, men mind their own business—usually."

Brown stroked his cheek with a calloused thumb. "Suit yourself. Here's the set-up, then. It's strictly confidential, or the deal's off. You'll know why later. Anyhow—we want you to guide us into the Black Forest."

* * * *

Garth's laughter rang harsh and bitter. Brown and the girl watched him with impassive eyes.

"What's so funny about it?" she asked, scowling.

Garth sobered. "Nothing much. Only for five years I've been sweating blood trying to get into the Forest, and I know the place better than anybody on Ganymede. See this?" He rolled up his sleeve and exhibited a

11

purplish scar along his arm. "A cannibal-plant did that. I couldn't get away from the thing. Bullets and knives don't hurt the bloodsucker. I had to stand there for two hours, helpless, till it got all the blood it wanted. After that I managed to pull away."

"I've picked up a few scars myself," Brown said quietly.

Garth glared at him. "Not in the Black Forest. The only way to get through that pest-hole is with a big, armed expedition. Even then ... you ever heard of the Noctoli?"

"No. Who—"

"Flowers. Their pollen works funny—plenty funny. They grow in the interior, and they give you amnesia. Not even gas-masks help. The stuff works in through your skin."

"Doesn't it affect you?" the girl wanted to know.

Garth shivered and drank again. "It did—once. Later I managed to work out an antitoxin. And I've built up immunity, anyway. But it's quite a laugh. The two of you wanting to go into the Black Forest!"

Brown's face was emotionless. "With an expedition, well armed. I'll provide that."

"Oh. That's a bit different. Just the same—what are you after?"

"Just sightseeing," the girl said.

Garth grinned crookedly. "Okay. I know the stories. Everybody on Ganymede's heard of the *Ancients*."

Captain Brown's eyes hooded. "What about them?"

"The lost race? That they lived on Ganymede thousands of years ago, and had the greatest science ever known to the System. That they died, nobody knows how, and the secrets of their civilization were lost. Chahnn's only one of their ruined cities. There've been a dozen others found. And full of gadgets and robots that nobody knows how to work. There was a central power-source, but Earthmen have never figured out how it worked or what fuel was used. The inscriptions found in the cities didn't tell anything."

"Fair enough," Brown nodded. "Except you forgot one thing. You know the Ancient Tongue. You speak it."

Garth chewed his lip. "So what?"

"Where did you learn it?"

"I don't know. In the Black Forest, I suppose. I don't remember."

The girl made an impatient gesture. She quieted as Brown glanced at her.

"From the Zarno, Garth?"

"*I don't know!* There's no proof the Zarno even exist!"

"If you've gone far enough into the Black Forest—"

12

Garth said angrily, "Remember what I told you about the Noctoli? The effect of the pollen? When I got back to Oreport here I had amnesia. I—" He hesitated. "I don't remember. I never did remember what happened in the Black Forest."

"Um-m." Brown rubbed his cheek again. "A lost race of savages no outsiders have ever seen—a race speaking the tongue of the Ancients. How could they live around those Noctoli flowers of yours?"

"Natural immunity," Garth said. "Built up over a period of generations. I didn't have that—then."

* * * *

The girl leaned forward, ignoring Brown. "Mr. Garth," she said swiftly, "I think I'd better explain a bit more. Shut up, Carver!" She frowned at Brown. "There've been too many mysteries. Here's the set-up. I've got half of a—a map. It shows the location of something in the Black Forest that's immensely valuable—the greatest treasure the System's ever known. I don't know what it is. The original inscription, in the Ancient's language, is cryptic as the devil. But the Ancients thought this treasure important enough to be worth hiding in the Black Forest. They set the Zarno to guard it. See?"

Garth grunted. "So what?"

"Well—I'm Paula Trent, archaeologist. Not that it matters. For months Carver and I have been waiting our chance to fit out an expedition and come on here. We didn't have the money, at first, and when we did get it, the government refused us permission. We had no proof, they said, and the Black Forest is impenetrable. So we waited. A month ago we got wind of a research ship, the *Hunter*, coming on here to investigate Chahnn. The same old stuff—digging around in the ruins, trying to find out what made the machines and robots tick, trying to make sense out of the inscriptions. Trying to find a cure for the Silver Plague."

Garth said, "No cure's been found yet, then."

Paula shook her head. "No. Since it started on Earth ten years ago, it's wiped out one-twentieth of the population, and unless it's stopped, it'll destroy all life on our world. But that's old stuff. Except the government's sending out their best men to Ganymede, because it's known the Silver Plague existed here once and was conquered. The inscriptions in Chahnn show that. But they don't say what the treatment was, or give any hints. However—" She brushed red-gold hair from her forehead. "Carver and I have planted men in the *Hunter* crew. Tough, good men who'll strike out with us into the Black Forest. With equipment."

"Desertion, eh?"

"Technically, sure. But the only way. Nobody will listen to us. We know—we *know*—the Ancients hid their most valuable treasure in the

Black Forest. What it is we don't know. We're hoping it'll solve a lot of problems—the mystery of what powered their machines, what happened to the Ancients—all that."

"No planes can be used," Garth said. "There's no place to land in the Forest."

"That's why we want you. You know the Forest, and you know the Ancient Tongue. Guide the *Hunter* crew to Chahnn. Then, when we give the word—head for the Black Forest with us."

Garth said, "On one condition. You can't go."

Paula's eyes narrowed. "You're in no position to—"

"Men might get through. A woman couldn't. Take it or leave it," Garth repeated stubbornly.

Captain Brown nodded to the girl. "All right, it's a deal. Sorry, Paula, but he's on the beam. Here's ten bucks, Garth. Balance when we get to Chahnn. We leave tomorrow at Jupiter-rise."

* * * *

Garth didn't answer. After a moment Paula and Brown rose and went out through the mildewed tapestry curtain. Garth didn't blame them. The *Moonflower-Ritz* smelled.

Presently he found Tolomo and gave him the money. The Ganymedean hissed worriedly.

"Only ten?"

"You'll get the rest later. Gimme a bottle."

"I don't think—"

Garth reached across the bar and seized a quart. "Hereafter I do my drinking out-of-doors," he remarked. "I'll feel cleaner."

"*Sfant!*" Tolomo flung after him as he headed for the door. Garth's cheeks burned red at the word, which is Ganymedean and untranslatable; but he didn't turn. He stepped out into the muddy street, a cold wind, sulphurous and strong, stinging his nostrils.

He looked around at the collection of plastic native huts. Till the *Hunter* had arrived, he'd been the only Earthman in Oretown. Now—

He didn't feel like talking to natives. The Tor towered against the purple sky, where three of Jupiter's moons were glowing lanterns. At the base of the Tor was Garth's shack.

Swaying a little, clutching the bottle, he headed in that direction. He had waited five years for this moment. Now, when at last he might find the answer to the problem that had turned him into a derelict, he was afraid.

He went into his hut, switched on the radiolite, and stood staring at a door he had not opened for a long time. With a little sigh he pushed at the latch. The smell of musty rot drifted out.

14

A lamp revealed a complete medical laboratory, one that had not, apparently, been used for months at least. Garth almost dropped a bottle as he fumbled it from the shelf. Cursing, he opened the rotgut Ganymedean whiskey and poured it down his throat.

That helped. Steadied somewhat, he went to work. The Noctoli pollen antitoxin was still here, but it might have lost its efficacy.

He tested it.

Good. It seemed strong, the antibodies having a long life-cycle. It would work.

Garth packed a compact medical kit. After that he stood for quite a while staring at two blank spaces on the wall, where pictures had once hung.

Moira and Doc Willard.

Damn! Garth snatched up the liquor and fled the house. He fought his way along the steep path that led to the Tor's summit. The physical exertion was a relief.

* * * *

At the top, he sat down, his back against a rock. Beneath him lay Oretown, yellow-blue lights winking dimly. In a cleared field some distance away was the ovoid shape of the spaceship that had brought Paula and Brown—the *Hunter*.

To the west, across sandy desert, lay Chahnn, dead city that had once housed an incredibly-advanced science—lost now, its people dust. Northwest, beyond distant ridges, was the Black Forest, unexplored, secret, menacing.

Six years ago Dr. Jem Willard had come to Ganymede with his intern, Ed Garth. Willard was trying to discover the cure for the Silver Plague that was wrecking Earth. He would have found it—he had got on the track. But—

An emergency call had come in one night. A native needed an appendectomy. Willard couldn't fly a plane. He had called on Garth, and Garth had been drunk.

But he had piloted the plane anyhow. The crack-up happened over the Black Forest.

That was the last thing Garth remembered, or almost the last. It would have been more merciful if the oblivion had been complete. Months later he staggered out of the Forest into Oretown, alone. The Noctoli poison had almost erased his experiences from his mind. He could remember a bare cell where he and Willard had been prisoned—that, and one other thing.

A picture of Doc Willard stretched on an altar, while Garth lifted a gleaming, razor-sharp knife above his friend's breast.

He remembered that, but no more. It was enough.

The question burning in his brain had nearly wrecked his sanity. He had tried to get back into the Black Forest, to find Willard, dead or alive, to learn what had happened—to discover the answer to his problem. He had failed.

A year later he learned that his fiancée, Moira, had died of the Silver Plague. And he knew that Willard might have saved her, had he lived and continued his research.

After that, Ed Garth hit the skids. He went down fast, stopping only when he reached the bottom.

He killed the bottle and threw it out into emptiness, watching yellow light glint on glass as it dropped.

Well, he had his chance now. An expedition going into the Black Forest. But Garth was no longer the same husky giant who had fought his way through that deadly jungle. Five years on the skids had played havoc with him. Stamina was gone. And the Black Forest was as terrible, as powerful, as ever.

Garth wished he had brought another bottle.

CHAPTER II

Jupiter is a ball of luminous clouded marble, gigantic in the sky of Ganymede. Its light is a queer, pale glow that lacks the warm brilliance of sunlight. When the titanic planet lifts over the horizon, gravity seems to shift, and the ground feels unstable beneath your feet.

Jupiter was rising now. Oretown lay ugly and desolate in the strange dawn. Across the plain where the spaceship had landed a string of truck-cats, big silvery desert freighters, stood motionless, ready to start the trip. There were signs of activity. At the central port of the *Hunter* stood a lanky, gray-haired man with a clipped, stiff Van Dyke. Behind him was Captain Brown.

Garth, his medical kit strapped to his back, ploughed through the light film of snow that lay over the sand. He was shivering in his thin garments, wishing he had a drink. Neither Brown nor his companion saw Garth's approach. The gray-haired man was speaking.

"—time to start. If this guide of yours doesn't show up, we'll have to wait till we find another."

"He'll show up," Brown said. "I only gave him ten bucks."

Garth reached the foot of the ramp leading up to the port-valve. "'Morning. Am I late?"

There was no answer. He climbed the slope, slippery with snow despite the skid-treads, and stopped before the two men. Brown nodded at him.

"Here's our guide, Commander Benson."

Benson scowled incredulously under tufted brows. "What the devil! You—you're an Earthman!"

"Sure," Garth said. "What about it?"

The Commander glanced at Brown. "I expected a native. I didn't know —" He left the sentence hanging. "You can't wear those rags, man. Captain, break out some clothes for him." Without another look at Garth, Benson hurried down the ramp, shouting orders to someone below.

Brown grinned at the other. "Come on inside," he urged, and, in a lower tone, "He's the big shot. You know enough to keep your mouth shut —eh?"

Garth nodded. Brown peered at him sharply.

"You need coffee. I'll lace it. Come along." He took Garth to the galley, and, presently, supplied food, drink, and clothing. He lit a cigaret, idly watching the smoke sucked into the air-conditioning grill.

"Benson's a tough egg," he said at last. "If he had the slightest idea we were figuring on—what we're figuring on, there'd be trouble. The Commander never takes chances. We've got to give him the slip, somehow."

Garth gulped coffee. "How many men do you have?"

"Ten."

"Not many."

"Fully armed, though. There are sixty in the expedition altogether, but I could only feel sure of ten. Some of them I planted myself."

Garth took the cigaret Brown handed him. "Thanks ... I know Chahnn pretty well. Once we get there, we can get away from the others."

"How?"

"Underground passages—not well known. We'll come out about thirty miles from Chahnn, and from there it's another twenty to the Black Forest."

"The last lap on open ground?"

"Yeah."

"Not so good. If Benson misses us, he'll have planes out scouting. I've a hunch he's suspicious already."

"If he catches up with us, so what? There'll be other chances."

"That's what you think," Brown said grimly. "I told you Benson was a tough egg. He'd clap us all in the brig and we'd end up with prison sentences on Earth—hazarding the success of a planetary expedition, they call it. So you see why we've got to find this treasure, whatever it is."

"Then you don't know either, eh?"

"Maybe I've a few ideas.... Finished? Let's go, then." Brown came to his feet.

* * * *

Garth followed Brown out of the ship, pondering. The Ancients had, admittedly, been an incredibly advanced race. Any treasure they thought worth guarding would be plenty valuable. Gold? Gems? They seemed trivial, compared to the tremendous scientific powers of the Ancients. And unimportant as well, while the Silver Plague raged over Earth.

They moved along the string of truck-cats, each loaded with the necessary equipment, and reached the first. Commander Benson was already there, talking to the pilot. He looked around.

"Ready? What's your name—Garth? All right, get in."

The front compartment of the truck-cat was roomy enough. Paula Trent, Garth saw, was already there. She gave no sign that she noticed him. He shrugged and found a seat, and Captain Brown dropped beside him, impassive as ever.

The pilot came in. "Sit up here, next to me, buddy," he ordered. "I'll need your help wrestling this tank through the arroyos."

Benson himself was the last man to enter. He slid the door shut and nodded.

"Warm her up."

Beside the driver, Garth could not see the others, nor could he hear their conversation as the motors coughed and snarled into life. The truck-cat lurched forward on her caterpillar treads. The pilot looked inquiringly at Garth.

"Where'll I head? West? What about these quicksands I've been hearing about?"

"Steer for that mountain peak 'way over there," Garth told him. "It's easy to see the sink-holes. They're big grey patches on the sand, with no snow on 'em."

The roar of the engine died into a monotonous murmur. It was possible to hear the conversation in the rear of the compartment. Commander Benson was talking.

"—atomic power. It must have been that; there's no other answer. All we need to know is the nature of the booster charge."

"I don't get it," Paula said. "Booster charge?"

"As far as our physicists know, atomic power's possible if there's a known way to start it and control it. Earth's reserves are nearly exhausted. Oil, coal—used up almost completely. And Earth needs power plenty bad, to maintain civilization."

"The other planets have fuel."

"Spaceshipping's too expensive. It's prohibitive, Paula. Unless a new power source is found very soon, Earthmen may have to migrate to another world—and our civilization's so complex that that's nearly impossible. Maybe we can find the answer in Chahnn this time. It was one of the biggest cities of the Ancients."

"I've never seen it," Captain Brown said.

* * * *

Benson grunted. "I did, once. Years ago. Tremendous! The scientific achievements they must have had! And nobody knows what happened to the Ancients. They just vanished, and their machines kept running till they'd used up their power—and stopped. So there's no trace left. We've located the fuel chambers, but in every case they've been empty. Experiments have been made—unsuccessfully."

"You still think my translation of the Harro Panel was wrong, eh?" Paula put in.

19

"I do," Commander Benson said. "It was a variable cipher. No one else agrees with you that it was a code map."

"Ever heard of a double code?"

"I'm sorry," Benson said shortly. "We've settled all this. The Black Forest is impassable. We can't risk our chance of success on a wild goose chase."

Beside the pilot, Garth's mouth twisted sardonically. He had an idea, now, what Carver Brown and Paula were after. The secret of the Ancients' power-source. Well, it might be found in the Black Forest. Anything might. Including the lost race of the Zarno, and.... His eyes went hard. Not yet would he let himself believe Doc Willard was still alive. The most he could hope for was an answer to that question—the tormenting problem of whether or not he had killed Willard.

Lost in his absorption, he snapped out of it scarcely in time as the truck-cat skidded on slick ice.

"Hard left! Sand the treads!" Instinctively his hand flashed to the right lever, releasing a sprinkling of sand that provided traction. He held it down while the pilot fought the wheel. They lurched, swung half around, and found level surface again. Through the window Garth could see a twenty-foot-wide funnel, sloping down to a black hole at the center.

"What was it?" the pilot asked.

"*Creethas*, the natives call 'em, but that doesn't mean much. Six-foot insects. Poisonous. They dig traps like ant-lions on Earth, pits with sloping sides. Once you skid on the ice, you slip on down to the hole at the bottom."

"Dangerous?"

"Not to us, in here. But we might have damaged the engine."

"Keep your eyes open after this, Garth," Commander Benson said sharply.

"Okay." Garth was silent. The truck-cat drove on, leading the procession.

The vehicles were fast. On level ground they raced, hitting eighty m.p.h. sometimes. By Jupiter-set they had reached Chahnn. Paula, for one, was disappointed.

"I expected a city," she told Garth as they stared around at the mile-square block of black stone, raised a few feet above ground level, its surface broken by a few structures oddly reminiscent of the subway kiosks of two centuries ago.

"It's all underground," Garth said. He was feeling shaky, needing a shot or two of liquor. But there was none. In lieu of it, he borrowed a cigaret from the girl and idled about, watching the men make camp.

* * * *

20

The roomy truck-cats provided accommodations for sixty men without crowding. It wasn't necessary to set up tents. Indeed, in that icy air, only "warmer" tents, heated by induced current in their metallic fabric, would have been feasible. The trucks, however, could be heated easily and were air-conditioned. Garth walked over to a kiosk and peered into the black depths. Chahnn lay below, the gigantic, complicated city of the Ancients.

Through Chahnn was the road to the Black Forest—the only road they could use, under the circumstances.

Garth shivered and went in search of Brown. He was feeling shakier than ever. Vividly in his mind was a picture he did not want to remember —a man stretched on an altar, a knife at his breast....

He found Brown beside one of the trucks, looking into the darkness.

"Captain—"

"Huh? Oh, Garth. Say, Paula—Miss Trent took a flashlamp and went down into Chahnn to do a bit of exploring. I was thinking of going after her. Any danger down there?"

Garth shook his head. "It's a dead city. She'll be okay."

"Unless she gets lost."

"She won't. There are markers pointing to the outlets. How about a drink? I could use one."

Scowling, Brown nodded and pushed Garth into the truck. "I bunk in here, with the Commander. You'll have to find a place with the men, somewhere. Oh, by the way—" He pushed folded slips into Garth's hand. "Here's the rest of that forty. And here's a drink."

Garth gulped brandy better than any he had tasted in years. He didn't bother with a glass. Brown watched him with an almost imperceptible curl of the lip.

"Thanks.... When do I get that ten thousand?"

"When we're back here. I don't trust you quite enough to let you have it now."

Garth wiped his mouth with the back of his hand, considered, and drank again. "I won't run out on you. You're after that Ancients' power-source, aren't you?"

Brown's eyes narrowed a bit. "Any of your business?"

"Not in the way you mean. But I know the Black Forest. I might be able to give you some ideas, if I'm not left too much in the dark. Still, I can guess a little. I know you expect to run into the Zarno."

"Yeah?"

Garth made an impatient gesture. "Hell, why did you want me as a guide? It wasn't only because I knew the Forest. I can speak the Ancient Tongue—the same language the Zarno are supposed to use. You'll want me to palaver with them."

21

"Maybe." Brown went to the back of the truck and found a fresh pack of cigarets. "We can talk about that later."

"We ought to talk now. I know what sort of equipment you'll need in the Forest. If you run out on Benson half-equipped, it'll be just too bad."

The door swung open, admitting a blast of frigid air. Commander Benson stepped in, his lips tight and hard, his eyes blazing. Brown, at the end of the chamber, swung around, a sudden, surprised tenseness in his attitude.

"I don't think you'll do any running out on me, Captain," Benson said.

Brown flashed Garth a glance. "Damn you," he half-whispered. He took a step forward, tigerishly menacing.

* * * *

Benson pulled a gun from his pocket. "Don't move," he said. "Hold it —right there. I thought you'd given up that crazy idea you and Paula had, but apparently—" He shrugged. "Well, I'll have to put you and the girl under guard. No one in this outfit's heading for the Black Forest if I can help it."

Brown's hand hovered in midair.

"Don't try it," Benson said. "Keep your gun where it belongs. The sound of a shot wouldn't help you any." He stepped back, his mouth opening in a shout that would summon others.

Brown, at the other end of the truck, could not have reached him in time, but the Commander had forgotten or ignored Garth. That was a mistake. Garth was only a few feet from Benson, and he galvanized into unexpected action. He sprang, one hand clamping over the gun, the other, clenched, driving in a hard, short jab at Benson's chin.

There was strength in that punch, and it connected at the right point. Had Garth not been gripping the Commander's hand, the latter would have gone backward, out of the truck.

"Knockout!" Brown said tonelessly. He was suddenly beside Garth, yanking Benson forward. "Shut the door. Quick."

Garth obeyed. Turning, he saw the Captain kneeling beside Benson's motionless form. After a moment Brown looked up.

"He'll come out of it soon. Maybe too soon. Get me those straps from the corner."

Garth did that, and then had another drink. He felt lousy. He watched Brown bind the Commander and thrust the lax figure out of sight, under a bunk.

"That does it," Brown said, rising. "We're in the soup now. But—it was lucky you hit him when you did."

"What now?"

"We start for the Black Forest before Benson wakes up. I'm second in command. I'll get my own men, and we'll jump the gun." Brown's eyes were excited.

"Equipment?"

"We'll take what we can. Weapons, mostly. Stay with me."

They went out of the truck into the soft light of four moons, two large, two tiny. Fourfold shadows paced them over the icy slick. Garth hurried off to find his medical kit. By the time he returned, Brown had mustered his men and was waiting. He gave Garth a brief glance.

"Okay. Morgan—" He turned to a giant in uniform. "I'll be back in a couple of hours. As soon as we find Miss Trent. 'Bye."

"'Bye, sir."

Garth led the way into one of the kiosks. Lamps were flashed on. A spiral ramp led steeply down.

In an undertone Brown said, "I told Morgan Commander Benson sent me to find Paula Trent—that she was lost in the city. So we're safe till—"

"We're safe till we leave the underground passage," Garth said. "After that, twenty miles across open ground. Has Benson got planes?"

"Portable ones, yeah."

"Then we'd better do that twenty miles at night."

The ramp ended. Before them was a gigantic room where their tiny lamps were lost. Here and there enigmatic shadows loomed, the dead, fantastic machines of the Ancients that had once made Chahnn alive and powerful.

* * * *

Garth went directly to an opening in the wall, Brown and his ten men following, and entered a short tunnel. At one spot he paused, ran his finger over a panel of smooth metal, and pressed. A black oval opened silently.

"Here's the way. They won't follow us beyond this point."

Brown nodded. "Sampson, get the men inside. Wait here for me. I'll be back as soon as I can."

A burly, beak-nosed fellow with a cast in one eye and flaming red hair saluted casually. "Right. Come on, boys. Hop through. Mind your packs."

Garth stared at Brown. "What d'you mean? Where—"

The Captain said, "We're taking Paula Trent with us."

"No! It's nearly suicide for us—she couldn't make it at all."

"She's tougher than you think. Besides, she's got the map. And she's an archaeologist. I can't read the Ancients' lingo. Can you?"

Garth shook his head. "I can speak it, that's all. But—"

"If we find what we're after, we'll need Paula Trent. She's down here somewhere. Let's go find her."

23

"I tell you—"

Brown brought out a gun and leveled it.

"Find her. Or I'll find her myself, and we'll head for the Black Forest without you. Because you'll be dead. I haven't come this far to let you stop me. And chivalry looks a bit funny on a guy like you."

Sudden murder-light flared in the pale eyes.

"Find her!" Brown whispered. "And—fast!"

CHAPTER III

Garth knuckled under. There was nothing else to do. He knew Brown wouldn't hesitate to kill him, and, after all, what the devil did Paula Trent mean to him? Her life was unimportant, compared to the hopeless quest that had quickened in his mind, despite himself.

For Doc Willard might still be alive. Even if he wasn't, there was that notebook the Doc had always carried around with him—a book that contained the medico's theories about the Silver Plague. Even if that ghastly dream-like memory were not merely delirium—even if Garth, witless and unknowing, had killed Willard—there was always that dim, desperate chance that the cure for the Plague might be found in the Black Forest.

So—damn Paula Trent! She didn't matter, when the lives of millions might depend on Garth's penetrating the jungle that had baffled him for five years.

Without a word he turned and started back, Brown keeping close beside him. The huge chamber loomed before them, filled with its cryptic shadows. There was time now to see what they had missed in their quick flight a few moments ago—though not much time, for pursuit might start at any minute.

Dead silence, and darkness, broken by the crossing beams of the brilliant lamps. Garth listened.

"Hear anything?"

Brown shook his head.

"Nothing."

"Okay. We'll try this way."

Then went into a passage that sloped down, ending in a vaulted room larger than the first. Brown swung up his gun abruptly as a figure seemed to leap from blackness in the ray of the lamp. Garth caught his arm.

"Robot. Unpowered. They're all over the city."

The robots—slaves of the Ancients, Garth thought, who had died with them, lacking the fuel that could quicken them to life. No Earthly scientists had ever been able to analyze the construction of the machines, for they were built of an alloy that was apparently indestructible. Acid and flame made no impression on the smooth, glittering black surface.

This one, like all the others, was roughly man-shaped, nearly eight feet tall, and with four arms, the hands extended into limber jointed fingers almost like tendencies. From the mask-like face complex glassy eyes stared blankly. It stood motionless, guarding a world that no longer needed guardians.

With a little shrug Garth went on, his ears alert for sounds. From the walls bizarre figures in muraled panels watched. Those murals showed a world of incredibly advanced science, Garth knew. He had seen them before. He spared them not a glance now.

The machines—

What were they? They loomed like dinosaurs in the endless chain of high-domed vaults. They had once given Chahnn power and life and strength. The murals showed that. The Ancient Race had used antigravity —a secret unknown to Earthmen—and they had created food by the re-arrangement of atomic patterns, not even requiring hydroponic tank cultures. They had ruled this world like gods.

And they had passed with no trace, leaving only these silent monuments to their greatness. With the power of the Ancients, Earth's lack of fuel-reserves would not matter. If the secret of atomic power could be found again, these machines would roar into thundering life—and machines like them would rise on Earth.

Power and greatness such as civilization had never known! Power even to reach the stars!

And—Garth thought wryly—a power that would be useless unless a cure for the Silver Plague could be found.

* * * *

He was almost running now, his footsteps and Brown's echoing hollowly in the great rooms. Silently he cursed Paula Trent. There were other levels below, many of them, and she might be down there—which would make the task almost impossible.

A distant flicker of light jerked Garth to a halt. He switched off his lamp, motioning for Brown to do the same.

It came again, far away, a firefly glimpse.

"Paula?" the Captain said.

"Guess so. Unless they're after us already."

"Take it easy, then."

They went on, running lightly on their toes. The light had vanished, but Garth knew the way. Suddenly they came out of a short tunnel into one of the great rooms, and relief flooded Garth as he saw Paula's face, pale in reflected light, a dozen feet away.

Simultaneously a faint sound came rhythmically—like dim drums.

Garth said sharply, "Hear that? Men coming down a ramp. Get the girl and let's go!"

26

But Paula was already coming toward them, blinking in the glare. "Who's that? Carver? I—"

Brown gripped her arm. "There's no time to talk now, Paula. We're in a jam. Keep your mouth shut and come along. Garth, can you get us back to that secret passage?"

"Maybe. It'll be blind luck if we make it. Turn your lamps out and link hands. Here." He felt Paula's firm, warm palm hard against his, and remembrance of Moira was suddenly unexpectedly painful. He had not seen an Earthgirl for years....

What of it, now? Garth moved cat-footedly forward, leading the others. He went fast. Once or twice he clicked on his light briefly. They could hear the noise of the search-party now, and a few times, could see distant lights.

"If they find that open panel—" Brown whispered.

"Keep quiet."

Garth pressed them back into an alcove as footsteps grew louder. Luck stayed with them. The searchers turned off at another passage. After that—

It was like a nightmare, a blind, stumbling race through the blackness of Chahnn, with menace hiding everywhere. Garth's hand was slippery with perspiration against Paula's by the time he stopped, his light clicking on and off again almost instantly.

"This is it," he said. "The panel's shut."

"Good. Sampson must have had sense enough to close it. Unless—"

Garth found the spring and pressed it. He flashed his light into the darkness, to see the familiar faces of Brown's men staring at him. The Captain thrust him forward. Paula was instantly beside him, and then Brown himself was through the oval gap.

"They're coming," he murmured. "How in hell does this work?"

"Here." Garth didn't use his light. Under his deft fingers the panel slid back into place, shutting off the noise of approaching steps. He gasped a little with relief.

"Okay," he said in a natural voice. "These walls are sound-proof. We can use our lights. We'll have to."

"What happened?" Paula's voice said. "You said we were in a jam, Carver. Well?"

"We'll talk as we go. Garth, you first. Paula, stay with me. Sampson, bring up the rear, will you?"

* * * *

Garth obediently set out down the sloping tunnel, scarcely listening to Brown's explanation. There were side branches to the passage here and there. He had to use his memory, which seemed less accurate than he remembered. Once he almost blundered, but caught himself in time.

Brown said, "Garth, we've got thirty miles of tunnel and twenty more above ground till we hit the Forest. Right? This is rough going. We won't get out of here till daylight. So we'd better camp in the passage, at the other end, till tomorrow night."

"We don't have to do that," Garth grunted. "This isn't Earth. Jupiter won't rise for thirteen hours."

"The men have heavy packs." Brown shifted his own big one uncomfortably. "Fifty miles is quite a way. Still, the quicker we reach the Forest, the safer we'll be."

"There's a river." Garth's voice was doubtful. "We might use that."

"Would it help?"

"Yeah. But it's dangerous."

"Why?"

"Spouts. Geysers. The water's apt to explode under you any time. And there are big lizards—"

"Would it take long to make a raft?"

Garth shook his head. "*Lata*-trees are better than balsa, and they grow on the banks. Plenty of vines, too. But—"

"We'll do that, then," Brown said decisively. "Speed it up. We've got thirteen hours. We can make it, all right."

Garth didn't answer.

After that it was pure monotony, a dull driving march through a bare tunnel, up slopes and down them, till leg muscles were aching with fatigue. Garth dropped into a state of tired apathy. He had no pack to carry, but nev-

28

ertheless his liquor-soaked body rebelled at the unaccustomed exertion. But he knew that each step brought him closer to his goal.

The thoughts swung monotonously through his brain. Doc Willard. The notebook. The cure. The Plague. Maybe—maybe—*maybe!*

If he got through—if he found the notebook—if it had the cure—that was what he wanted, of course.

But suppose he also found the skeleton of Doc Willard on an altar, with a knife-hilt protruding from the ribs?

He couldn't have killed Doc consciously. That was unthinkable. Yet the damnable influence of the Noctoli pollen did odd things to a man's mind.

Doc Willard—Moira—the Silver Plague—

Half asleep, aching with exhaustion, he slogged ahead, moving like an automaton. And, whenever he slowed his pace, Brown's sharp voice urged him on faster.

Grudgingly the Captain allowed them rest periods. But by the time they reached the tunnel's end the men were panting and sweating, and both Paula and Garth were near exhaustion. Thirty miles at a fast pace, with only occasional rests, is wearing work.

* * * *

They emerged from the passage to find themselves on the slope of a rocky hillock. Low ridges rose around them, silhouetted in triple-moon-light. A whitish haze hung close to the ground, filling the hollows like shining water.

Instinctively Brown looked up. A meteor, drawn by the immense gravity of Jupiter, flamed across the sky—that was all. And that was a familiar enough sight.

Garth, reeling with fatigue, nodded. "River—down there. Half a mile. The fog's thicker—"

"Okay. Let's go."

This lap of the journey was nearly the hardest. But the low roar of the river steadily grew louder as they stumbled on, the luminous mist lapping their ankles, their knees, their waists. It closed above their heads, so that they moved in a ghostlike, shadowless world in which the very air seemed dimly lighted.

Trees were visible. Garth, almost spent, searched for a shelving beach, found it, and dropped in a limp heap. He saw Paula sink down beside him. The men threw off their heavy packs with relief.

Brown—the man was made of rawhide and steel!—said, "I'll need help to make a raft. The boys that feel tired can keep their eyes open for pursuit planes. I don't think the Commander would send out truck-cats at night, but he'll use searching planes."

"They can't see us in this fog," Paula said faintly.

"They could hear us, with their motors muffled. So we'll work fast. Garth!"

"Yeah. What?"

"What trees do we want?"

Garth pointed. "*Lata.* Like that one, over there. They're easy to cut down, and they float. You'll find tough vines all around here." He forced the words out with an effort. Brown mustered eight of his men, including the red-haired Sampson, and led them away. The sound of ringing axes presently drifted back.

Two others had been stationed on hillocks, above the low-lying fog, to watch for planes. Garth, alone with Paula, was almost too tired to be conscious of her presence. He heard her voice.

"Cigaret?"

"Thanks...." Garth took one.

"Sorry I can't offer you a drink."

"So am I," Garth grunted. He could feel her eyes on him. He drew the smoke deep into his lungs, exhaling luxuriously.

"Got a gun?"

"Yes. Why?"

"Oh—things come out of the river sometimes. Hunting water-lizards, carnivorous. You learn to sleep with one eye open on Ganymede."

"It's a funny world," Paula acknowledged. "Once it was highly civilized. Now it's gone back to savagery."

"Conditions are bad here. Too vigorous. Jupiter gives light but not much heat. Animals and plants have to be tough to survive. This is summer-season, but it's plenty cold."

"How much do you know about the Zarno?" she asked abruptly.

Garth blinked. "Not much. Why?"

"Not many people have ever seen them. I'm wondering. I managed to translate some inscriptions from Chahnn.... The Zarno aren't human, are they?"

Garth didn't answer. Paula went on.

"The Ancients knew them, though. They tried to educate them—like Rome colonizing savage races. That's probably why the Zarno are supposed to speak the Ancient Tongue."

"They do."

"And then the Ancients died out—somehow. The Zarno were left. They became barbarous again. I wish I knew what they were like. Natives who've seen them don't seem able to describe the creatures. They wear shining armor, don't they?"

* * * *

30

Garth closed his eyes, trying to remember. A vague, dim picture was growing in his mind—man-like figures that glowed, faces that were craggy, hideous creatures....

"I've seen them," he said, "but I've forgotten. The Noctoli poison—it wrecked my memory."

"You don't recall anything?"

"I—" Garth rubbed his forehead. "Not human—no. Creatures like living statues, shining and moving.... I don't know."

"Silicate life?" Paula theorized thoughtfully. "It's possible. And it might evolve on a planet where conditions are so tough for survival. Such creatures wouldn't be affected by the Noctoli pollen, either, would they?"

"No. Or they've built up resistance. The virus is active only in daylight, when the flowers are open. I don't know why. Before we go too far into the Black Forest I'll have to give everyone antitoxin shots—everyone but me. The pollen doesn't work on me any more."

They were silent, resting. It seemed only a moment before Brown appeared, announcing that the raft was ready.

"It's a makeshift job, but it's strong," he said. "Listen, Garth, what about the planes spotting us on the river? We'll be an easy target."

"They wouldn't fire on us?"

"No. But they'd use sleep-gas, and nab us when we drifted ashore. We don't want that."

Garth rose, his muscles aching. "It's a chance. Most of the time there'll be fog on the river. That'll help." He found his medical kit and shouldered it. "I'm ready."

The men were already on the raft, a big platform of light, tough *lata*-logs bound together by vines. Garth took his place near the pile of equipment in the center. "Keep to midstream," he cautioned. "Watch for bubbles breaking ahead. Swing wide of those. Waterspouts."

The raft slid out from the bank, long poles guiding it. Water washed aboard and slipped away as the platform found its balance. Presently they were drifting downstream in the dimly-lighted fog, the black river murmuring quietly beneath them.

Garth kept his gaze ahead. It was hard to see in the faint, filtered light of the moons, but a ray-lamp would have been betraying to any planes that might be searching above.

"Swing left. Hard," he called.

The men obeyed. Oily bubbles were breaking the surface. As the raft moved toward the bank, a sudden geyser burst up from the river, a spouting torrent that tipped the platform dangerously and showered its occupants with icy spray.

Garth met Brown's eyes. "See what I mean?" he remarked.

"Yeah. Still, if that's all—"

The river flowed fast. Once or twice the plated back of a giant saurian was visible, but the water-reptiles did not attack, made wary, perhaps, by the bulk of the raft. There were other waterspouts, but the men soon became adept at avoiding them.

Sometimes they drifted through fog, sometimes the mists were dissipated by winds, though not often. During one of the latter periods a faint droning drifted down from above. It was the worst possible timing, for the two larger moons were directly overhead, blazing down on the river. The stub-winged shape of a plane loomed against the starry sky.

Brown said sharply, "Drop flat. Don't move." He forced Garth and Paula down. "No, don't look up. They'd see our faces."

"They can't miss us," Sampson muttered.

"There's fog ahead."

The sound of the plane's motors grew louder. Abruptly there was a splash. Another. Something shattered on the raft.

"Hold your breath!" Brown snapped.

Garth tried to obey. A stinging ache had crept into his nostrils. His lungs began to hurt. The plane had spotted them—that was obvious. Sleep-gas works fast.

Another soft crash. Garth scarcely heard it. He saw a stubby, cruciform shadow sweep over the raft, as the plane swooped, and then the wall of silvery fog was looming up ahead. Paula gave a little gasp. Her body collapsed against him.

The fire in Garth's chest was blazing agony. Despite himself, he let breath rush into his lungs.

After that, complete blackness and oblivion.

CHAPTER IV

Garth woke in reddish, dim twilight. Instantly he knew where he was, even before he sat up and saw the black boles of immense trees rising like pillars around him. The Forest!

"About time," Captain Brown's toneless voice said. "That sleep-gas put you under for hours."

Garth rose, glancing around. They were camped in a little clearing among the gigantic trees, and some of the men were heating their rations over radiolite stove-kits. From above, the crimson light filtered vaguely from a leafy roof incredibly far. The trees of the Black Forest were taller than California sequoias, and Jupiter-light reached the ground faintly, through the ceiling of red leaves that roofed the jungle. Paula, Garth saw, was lying with her eyes closed not far away.

"She all right?"

"Sure," Brown said. "Resting is all. We got away from Benson's plane —hit that fog-bank just in time. You'd passed out, so I took a chance and kept going. After we reached the Forest, I landed the raft and headed inland a bit. So here we are."

Garth nodded. "That was wise. The river goes underground a half mile further. Any—accidents?"

Brown looked at him oddly. "This might be Yosemite, for all the danger I've seen so far. It's a picnic."

"That," Garth said, "is just why it's so bad. You don't see the trouble till after it's happened." He didn't explain. "Where's my kit?"

"Here. Why?"

"Before we go any further, we'll need shots. Antitoxin against the Noctoli pollen. The flowers don't grow on the edges of the Forest, but the wind carries their poison quite a ways sometimes." Garth rummaged in his kit, found sealed vials and a hypo, and carefully sterilized everything over a radiolite stove he commandeered from one of the men. After that, he administered the antivirus, first to Paula and last of all to Brown. He took none himself; he had acquired a natural immunity to the pollen.

There was barely enough to go around. Brown's shot was slightly less than the regular dosage, which vaguely worried Garth. But the Captain, annoyed by the delay, was anxious to talk about immediate plans.

"Benson might land at the edge of the Forest and come after us a mile or so. Not further. But we'd better start moving." He led Garth over to where Paula sat. "It's time for you to see the map."

The girl nodded in agreement. She took out a folded flex-paper and extended it. Garth squinted down in the red twilight.

"Map?"

"More like a treasure hunt," Paula explained. "There's a series of guide-points, you see. So far we're okay—*narva* means west, in the Ancient Tongue, doesn't it?"

"*Narva.*" Garth gave the word a slightly different pronunciation. "Yeah. Well—three *sallags* northwest to the Mouths of the Waters Below —"

"Mouths of the Singing Below, I made it."

Garth shook his head. "I can't read the stuff. I just know the spoken language. Read the whole thing out loud, so I can get it."

Paula obeyed. Her pronunciation made some words unfamiliar to Garth, but by experiment he found what was meant.

"Uh-huh. A *sallag* is less than three miles, as far as I can judge. I think I know the place. It's a hill honeycombed with little caves. You can hear water running underneath it."

"That fits," the girl agreed. "This won't be so hard, after all."

Garth grunted. He turned to Brown.

"I want a gun. And a knife. I'll need both."

"Sampson!"

The red-haired man approached, squinting. "Yeah?"

"Rustle up a knife and gun for Garth."

"Check."

Paula was staring at Garth. "You expect trouble, don't you?"

"I do."

She made a gesture. "This all seems so peaceful—"

* * * *

"Listen," Garth said, "the Black Forest is the worst death-trap in the System. Here's why. The struggle for existence is plenty tough here. Brute strength isn't enough, nor agility. A tiger or a deer wouldn't last long here. In the Forest, the survival of the fittest means the plant or animal that can get the most food. That sort of thing has been going on here for a million years. The beasts developed super-quick reactions. They could smell danger a mile away. So they had to have strength, agility, and something else —to get close to their prey."

Brown stared. "What?"

"Invisibility. Or its equivalent. Ever heard of protective coloration? Camouflage? Well, the creatures of the Forest are the most perfect camou-

34

flage experts that exist. They don't simply trick your eyes, either. They trick the other senses. If you smell perfume, take it easy, or you'll find yourself asleep, while your head's being chewed off by a lizard that looks as nasty as it smells good. If you see a path and it feels solid, don't walk too far on it. Things have made that path. A carnivorous moss that feels exactly like smooth dirt underfoot—till their digestive juices start working. If you hear me yelling your name, take it easy. There are birds like harpies here that imitate sounds the way parrots do."

Garth's grin was tight. "You'll find out. It's camouflage carried to the last degree, for offense and defense. I know the Forest pretty well; you don't. You haven't developed a sort of sixth sense—an instinct—that tells you when something smells bad, even though it looks like a six-course dinner."

"All right," the Captain said. "This is your territory, not mine. It's up to you."

It was, Garth decided later as he led the way through the black columns of the trees, very much up to him. Brown and the others were tough, hard fighters, but they didn't know the subtleties of this hell-hole, where death lurked everywhere disguised. He had got a drink from Sampson and his nerves were less jagged, but physical exhaustion still gripped him. He'd been on the skids for a long time, and was in rotten bad shape. But if the girl could stand it, he could.

It was warmer in the Forest; the trees seemed to exhale heat and moisture, and there was no snow on the ground. Great ebony pillars of giant trees, rising hundreds of feet into the air, made the place a labyrinth. And the deceptive reddish twilight made walking difficult, even to Garth's trained senses.

There was trouble, though. When a gorgeously-colored butterfly, flame-red and green, fluttered down toward Paula, Garth hastily slapped at the insect with a thick leaf he was carrying. "Watch out for those," he told the girl, nodding toward the crushed body. "They're poisonous. Bad medicine."

And once, as Brown was about to seat himself on a rounded grayish boulder, Garth whirled the man away just in time. A hole in the rock gaped open, and a pair of fanged mandibles snapped out, clicking together viciously. Garth put a bullet in the thing. It heaved itself up on spidery legs, revealing that the "rock" was a carapace covering an insect-like body. And it took a long time to die.

There were other, similar incidents. They had a bad effect on the men, even Sampson. The crew Brown had picked was tough, but the Black Forest was like distilled poison. It was easier to face a charging rhino than to travel through this ebony jungle where silent, secret death lurked concealed, in a diabolic masquerade.

That was the first day. The second was worse. The trees were thicker, and sometimes it was necessary to use *machete*-blades to hew through the tangled undergrowth.

* * * *

Another day—and another—and another, following the clues on Paula's cipher map. They found the first guidepost, the hill honeycombed with caves, and from there went on to the east, camping at the edge of a ravine that dropped away into unplumbed darkness.

Camouflage-moss grew here, looking deceptively like solid ground. One of the men ventured too close to the edge of the cleft, and the moss crumbled beneath him, dropping him into a nest of the roots—twining, writhing cannibalistic serpents with sucker-disks that drank blood thirstily.

They got him out in time, luckily. But the men's nerves were jolted.

After that, day after day, constant alertness was vital. The party walked with guns and knives in their hands. Their footsteps rang hollow in the dead, empty silence of the Forest....

It was only Garth's knowledge of the dark wilderness that got them through to the interior. After a week, he was further in than he had ever penetrated before, except when he had crashed the air-car with Doc Willard five years ago.

But they were getting closer—nearer! More and more often Garth remembered the black notebook that might hold the cure for the Silver Plague. For some indefinable reason he had come to feel that Paula's goal was also his.

It was logical enough. They were searching for a lost treasure-house of the Ancient Race, guarded, perhaps, by the Zarno. And Garth was certain that, during that period of partial amnesia, he and Willard had been captives of the Zarno. He had been drugged with the Noctoli poison by day, but at night he had wakened in a bare cell with his friend—a cell with walls of metal, he recalled. It had been windowless. Lighted by a faint glow from one corner.

It checked. A ruin, once built by the Ancients, now inhabited by the Zarno.

If he could find that notebook—

He always stopped there. He knew what he might also discover—the skeleton of Willard, stretched on an altar. That picture always made his stomach go cold and tight.

That night Brown complained of a splitting headache. They camped near a stream, and Garth accompanied the Captain down to the bank, with canvas pails. Jupiter was invisible—they had not seen the sky for a week—but the red light was fading.

"Not too close," Garth cautioned. "Let me test it first."

Brown stared at him. "What now? I'm getting to expect anything here." The man's expressionless face showed signs of strain and exhaustion. He had no nerves, apparently, but the gruelling journey had told on him nevertheless.

Garth used his knife to cut down a sapling. He impaled a leaf on its point and extended it gingerly over the dark water. After a moment he felt a shock like a striking fish, and the pole was nearly wrenched from his hands. And he wrestled with it, Brown's hands gripped the sapling.

"What the devil! Garth—"

"Let it go. I was only testing, anyway." The pole was dragged into the water, where it thrashed about violently for a few moments.

"What is it?"

* * * *

Garth was searching through the underbrush for something. "Watersnakes. Big ones—perfectly transparent. They wait for some animal to come along and take a drink. Then—bang!" He nodded. "Here we are. We'll find a lot of the Noctoli flowers from now on."

He brought out a bloom nearly a foot in diameter, with leaves of pulpy, glossy black, a thick powdering of silver in its cup. "This is Noctoli, Captain. Looks harmless, doesn't it?"

"Yeah." Brown rubbed his forehead. "The pollen gives you amnesia?"

"In the daytime, when it's active. It's phototropic—needs light. Jupiter can't have set yet, so this ought to work." Garth found another pole, speared the flower on its tip, and extended the blossom over the water. He shook the silver dust into the stream.

"It works fast. The snakes will be paralyzed in a few seconds. The current carries off the pollen, we dip up the water we need—and that's that."

Paula appeared through the bushes, glancing around warily. In the last week everyone had learned to be alert always. Lines of fatigue showed on her pale face. Red-gold hair was plastered damply on her forehead.

"Carver—"

"What's up?"

She glanced at Garth, "The men. Sampson's talking to them."

Brown's rat-trap mouth clamped tight. "That so? Sampson shoots off his mouth too much. What's the angle?"

"I think they want to go back."

Garth, dipping up water in the canvas buckets, said, "We've only three more days to go, unless we run into bad country."

"I know. But—they're armed."

"I'll talk to 'em," Brown said quietly. He lifted two of the pails and started up the path, Paula and Brown trailing him. Presently they reached the clearing where camp had been made.

The men weren't cooking. Instead, they were gathered in a knot around Sampson, whose blazing red hair stood up like a beacon. Brown put down his burden and walked toward them.

They broke up at sight of him, but didn't scatter. Sampson's hand crept imperceptibly toward his holster.

"Trouble?" Brown asked.

Sampson squinted at him. "No trouble. Except we didn't know the Forest would be as bad as it is."

"So you want to go back?"

"You can't blame us for that," Sampson said, hunching his heavy shoulders. "It's only dumb luck that's kept us alive so far. We didn't bargain for this, Captain."

"I told you what to expect."

"All you said was that it'd be dangerous. None of us knew the Forest. Those damn bloodsucker plants are the worst. They reach out at a guy everywhere he turns. And the other things—we can't get through, Captain! You ought to be able to see that yourself!"

"Nobody's been killed so far."

"Blind luck. And Garth, too. He knows this country. If we didn't have him, we wouldn't have lasted a day."

"We've got him," Brown said crisply. "So we're going on. Only three more days, anyhow. That's enough. Start cooking your rations." He turned his back on Sampson and walked away. The red-haired giant hesitated, scowling. Finally he shrugged and glanced around at the others.

That broke the tension. One by one the men scattered to prepare food.

Only Garth was gnawed by a persistent, deep-rooted fear. He didn't admit it, even to himself. But he watched Brown closely that night, and finally unpacked his medical kit and carefully searched it for something he knew wasn't there.

He was dreading the next morning.

CHAPTER V

Slow reddish dawn brightened over the Forest. Garth felt someone shaking him. He grunted, stirred, and opened his eyes to see Paula's white face, and, behind her, Sampson.

"Yeah. What's wrong?" He scrambled out of his blankets, blinking. The girl, pale to the lips, pointed toward a recumbent figure.

"Carver. Captain Brown. He's—I don't know!"

Sampson said gruffly, "Looks like he's dead. The men on guard duty said he didn't move once all night."

Icy bands constricted suddenly around Garth's heart. Without answering he got his kit and went over to examine Brown. The man lay motionless, his breathing normal, but a deep flush on his brown cheeks.

"It isn't the Plague, is it?" Sampson asked, his voice not quite under control.

Garth shook his head. "Hell, no! It's—" He hesitated.

Paula caught his arm. "What? Some insect poisoned him—one of those butterfly-things?"

Garth carefully repacked his kit. He didn't look up.

"He's got a dose of the Noctoli pollen. That's all. It's not fatal. He'll come out of it after he leaves the Forest, or after he builds up immunity."

"How long would that take?"

"A month or more."

Garth bent over the apparently sleeping man. "Get up, Brown," he said insistently. "Hear me? Get up?"

The Captain stirred. His eyes opened, blank and unseeing. He drew himself from his blankets and rose, looking straight ahead. Paula shrank back with a little gasp. There was a flurry of movement among the men in the background.

"He'll be all right tonight. The poison only works in the daytime—I've told you that."

"We can't march at night," Paula said. "Not—here!"

"I know. It's impossible. Our lights would attract the butterflies—and plenty of other things."

Sampson whirled on the others. "Pack your equipment! We're getting out of here, fast!"

39

They hurried to obey. Paula got in front of Sampson as he turned, and the giant stopped, blinking at her.

"You can't leave the Captain here, Sampson."

"We'll carry him, then. But we're getting out."

Garth moved to Paula's side. "You won't need a litter. He can walk. Noctoli poison works like hypnotism. You're semi-conscious, but your will's in abeyance. If anyone tells Brown to follow us, he'll do it."

Paula was biting her lip. "We can't go back now. We've only three days to go."

"Look," Sampson said grimly, "why in hell should we commit suicide? Suppose we head on for three days. We reach this lost city of yours, or whatever it is. What then? We're in the middle of the Black Forest. Another thirteen days to get out! It's too much of a gamble. We're leaving now, and you can come along or stay here—suit yourself!" He turned away.

* * * *

Left alone, Paula looked helplessly from the motionless, staring figure of Brown to Garth.

"Carver!"

He didn't move. Garth grinned wryly.

"He'll obey commands, that's all. He won't wake up till tonight."

Paula clenched her hands. "We've got to go on! We've got to! If we go back now—"

"Commander Benson will clap us in the brig, eh?"

She looked at him angrily. "It isn't only that. We'd lose our chance. You were right, Garth—we're after the power-source of the Ancients. The secret's hidden here, in the Black Forest. That cipher from Chahnn proved that—to me, anyway. Earth needs power, more than you can imagine. Without it, civilization will collapse—soon, too."

"Suppose we go on," Garth said slowly. "I didn't tell you this, but the reason the poison hit Brown was because my antitoxin was too old. He had a short dose, too. The other men—well, they'll go under themselves in a day or so. You, too."

Blue smudges showed under the girl's eyes. "Oh," she said after a moment. "So it's like that."

"Just like that."

Paula's stubborn chin tilted up. "I don't care—there's still a way. We'll be all right at night, you said. Well, we'll do our traveling and fighting by night."

"Fighting?"

"The Zarno. Garth, we've got to do it, somehow. Once we find that power-source, we can use it! There'll be weapons the Ancients left, I'm

40

sure of it. The murals at Chahnn showed they had weapons, strong enough to conquer the Zarno. If we can get those—"

"You're crazy," Garth said. "Plain crazy. What the hell do you expect me to do about it? Sampson would knock my block off if I tried to stop him now."

But he was thinking: we're losing more than a chance to find the Ancient's power-source. I'm losing my chance to find the cure for the Silver Plague.

"No," he said stubbornly.

Paula's lip curled. "I should have known better than to ask you for help. I'll handle this myself." She unholstered her gun.

Garth looked at her. She'd fail. She couldn't handle these ten hard-shelled fighters, headed by Sampson. She'd fail. And, in the end, she'd go back to Earth, in the brig, back to the certain death of the Silver Plague. Oh, it might miss her, of course. But it might not.

Paula would die as Moira had done, years ago.

Garth shrugged and slapped the girl's weapon down. "Stay out of this," he commanded, and turned away, walking across the clearing to where Sampson and the others were shouldering their kits.

The red-haired giant looked up at Garth's approach. "Step it up," he said. "We're in a hurry."

"I'm not going."

Sampson's furry brows drew together. "The hell you're not. We need you!"

There was a band of ice around Garth's middle. "I know that. You can't get through without me. You'll never get out of the Forest alive. That's tough. Paula and I are going ahead, with Captain Brown. We're finishing what we started."

"You lousy so-and-so!" Sampson roared. His big hand reached out, clutching. Garth stepped back, drawing his pistol.

"Take it easy," he said under his breath. But there was a gun in Sampson's hand now. Behind the giant, the other men stirred angrily.

"You're coming with us!"

"Not alive. I won't be much good to you dead, will I?"

After a moment Sampson re-holstered his gun. He looked around at the others.

Someone said, "We can get along without that son."

Sampson growled at him. "Shut up. We can't. You'd have been sucked dry by that spider-thing yesterday if Garth hadn't seen it in time. He knows where to walk in this hell-hole."

Garth didn't say anything. He waited, holding his gun with casual lightness.

Sampson glared. "What do you want, then?"

"I want you to keep going—finish what you started."

"Then what?"

"We may find weapons—and other things."

"Suppose we don't?"

"Then we'll come back. I got you in here, and I'm the only man on Ganymede who can get you out."

Sampson's eyes narrowed. "Suppose we say yes. You can't keep a gun on us all the time. We might jump you. There are ways of making a man do things he doesn't want to do."

"Sure," Garth admitted, "you could torture me. Only that wouldn't help."

Sampson's gaze flicked past to the girl. Garth said quickly, "That wouldn't help either. Here's why. The antitoxin I gave you was too old. It isn't working the way it ought. Captain Brown was the first man to go under. But within three days, at the latest, every damn one of you will have Noctoli poison!"

Garth thought Sampson was going to shoot him then and there. A yell went up from the men.

Sampson's lifted hand quieted them. The giant was pale under his spaceburn.

"Is that straight?"

Garth nodded. "It's on the beam. Yeah. It'll take you a week to get out of the Forest, and you won't last that long, even if you force me to guide you. I don't think you can do that, anyway. But even if you did—within three days you'll be like the Captain. Walking dead men! You'll be okay at night, but you can't travel at night. By day you'll be living statues, sitting in the Forest waiting for the bloodsucker plants to come along and drain your blood, waiting for the poisonous butterflies to paralyze you and lay their eggs under your skin, waiting—you've seen what sort of things live in the Forest. Every day you'll be helpless. You can't run. Some night you'll wake up with your legs chewed off, or the butterfly maggots eating you alive. Like that? Well, that's what you'll get—and I'm the *only* guy that can save you!"

* * * *

The faces of the men told Garth that his shots had gone home. The deadly menace of the forest, lurking always in the background, had worked into their nerves. Sampson's big hands clenched.

"Damn you!" he snarled. "You can't—"

Garth went on quickly. "I'm handing this to you straight. We're in a spot, sure, but we can get out of it. I can make more antitoxin, but it'll take a while. I can't do it while we're traveling. I need equipment. Here's what I'm proposing—we all keep going, the way we started. I'm immune to the pollen. If we move fast, we'll reach the lost city, or whatever it is, before you go under. Then I can start making antitoxin. We'll have to trap some small animals and allow time for incubation. But I'll be able to make fresh shots and neutralize the Noctoli pollen."

"It's too long a shot," Sampson said.

"Okay," Garth told him. "Suit yourself. Play it my way, or commit suicide." He turned and walked toward Paula, who had not moved from Brown's side.

Her eyes were steady on his. "Thanks. That was nice going—plenty nice, if you pull it off."

"It's suicide either way," Garth grunted. He began packing Brown's kit and his own.

Footsteps sounded. Garth didn't turn. He heard Sampson's deep voice, hoarse with repressed fear and rage.

"We're playing it your way, Garth. God help you if you make any boners!"

Sudden relief weakened Garth. He tried not to show it, though he realized that his hands were trembling.

"Fair enough," he said. "We'll march in ten minutes. Get the men ready."

Sampson muttered something and retreated. Garth slipped the pack on Brown's shoulders. The Captain, looking blankly ahead, didn't seem to notice.

"Keep your eye on him," Garth told Paula. "He'll be between us. He'll keep marching till we tell him to stop. See?"

She nodded, moistening her lips. "Y-yes. Is—that—going to happen to all of us?"

Garth said nothing. There wasn't anything to say.

But he knew, as he led the party away from the camp, how long a gamble he was undertaking. There were so many chances that he might fail! The odds were plenty tough—yet the stakes were equally high.

Had he known how difficult those odds were, Garth might not have risked it. For the Noctoli poison worked faster than he had guessed.

Meantime he guided ten sullen, fearful men, a walking corpse, and a girl deeper into the unexplored heart of the Black Forest. The Noctoli flowers breathed their poison from the underbrush, deadly and relentlessly.

CHAPTER VI

That day they met a new enemy: jet-black lizards, five feet long, that clung to the black tree-boles, perfectly camouflaged, till the party came close. Then the reptiles flashed toward them, fanged jaws gaping. Constant alertness was all that saved them—that, and the blazing guns that killed the monsters.

Presence of the lizards was no respite from the other perils. The bloodsucker plants were more numerous, and the camouflage-moss made deceptively inviting paths through the red gloom. By dark, everyone was nearly exhausted, nerves worn to rags. Garth knew it would not take much for the men to explode into furious resentment against him.

Luckily, an hour after they had made camp, Captain Brown woke from his drugged trance, perfectly normal. But it took a while to make him understand what had happened.

For the first time Garth saw Brown lose his iron self-control, and then it was only for a moment. A flash of stark horror showed on the Captain's lean, hard face, to be gone instantly.

He lit a cigaret, his eyes brooding on Paula and Garth. Briefly he glanced past them to the men, preparing their rations.

"Uh-huh. Not so good. I suppose it's useless to think of traveling by night."

"It's impossible," Garth told him.

"You can make more antitoxin?"

"Sure—but not here. It's too dangerous. We've been safe so far because we've moved fast, camping at a different spot every night. If we holed up, we'd have a gang of monsters down on us in no time."

Brown considered. "It's a nasty business, having my own body go back on me. A bit of a shock. Well—" He let smoke drift from his nostrils. "Two more days ahead of us, eh? Then we reach the lost city."

"If it is a city. We don't even know that."

"But we do know there may be Zarno around. We'll have to arrive there soon after dark, so I'll be ... conscious. If there's a fight, I want to be in on it. Why the devil didn't you test that antitoxin, Garth?" His voice was harshly angry.

Garth didn't answer. Brown had given him the rush act, but he wasn't making any excuses.

Paula said, "This isn't the best time to quarrel. You'd better talk to the men, Carver, so there'll be no trouble tomorrow."

"Yeah. Yeah, I suppose so."

Even the rebellious Sampson was convinced by Brown's well-chosen remarks.

They slept uneasily, with guards replaced every two hours, and the next day woke to find Captain Brown once more sunk into his Noctoli-trance. A few of the men complained of headaches.

By mid-morning Paula succumbed to the poison. Garth did not realize at first what had happened. Then, turning, he saw the girl's blank face and wide eyes fixed straight ahead as she marched along, and knew that she was entranced by the Noctoli till nightfall. The exercise of walking, speeding metabolism, had hastened the action of the virus.

They went on. An hour later another man went under. Then another. By noon only five men, including Garth and Sampson, were still conscious.

Their difficulties increased proportionately. They had to be on guard every second. The Noctoli victims walked quietly in line, but they did not react to danger. If the tentacles of a bloodsucker plant flashed out, they wouldn't try to escape. Their instinct of self-preservation had been dulled and blanketed.

The afternoon was pure hell. Garth, Sampson, and one other man had to guard and lead the rest. Their guns crashed incessantly, it seemed.

When they camped at the onset of darkness, Sampson and Garth alone remained.

* * * *

The red-haired giant, swaying on his feet, squinted at Garth, his face haggard with exhaustion.

"Nice going," he said sardonically, after a time. "What now? Maybe we'd better cut our throats."

Garth managed a shaky grin. "We're still okay. And there's only one more day left. Tomorrow—we'll make it then. We've got to."

Unwilling admiration showed in Sampson's eyes. "You're dead on your feet. I don't see how the hell you keep up this pace. Anyhow—we can't go back now. That's settled, anyway."

"Yeah. The others will wake up after a while. We'll have to stay on guard till then."

They did, guns drawn, peering at the silent depths of the Forest around them, while the rest of the party lay motionless, helpless against attack.

45

After a time Sampson spoke. Garth could not see his face in the heavy gloom.

"What are you after, Garth?"

"Eh?"

"I had you ticketed wrong. A beachcomber.... There must be something plenty important where we're going, or you wouldn't be so anxious to get there. What is it? Treasure, of course, but—jewels? Or what?"

Garth chuckled. "There may be. I don't know. Don't care."

"Hm-m." Sampson was silent, baffled. Garth's mind swung back to that ever-present question. Had he killed Doc Willard? Very soon, now, he might know the answer.

But that was important only to him. The vital point was the black note-book Doc had with him.

After a time Captain Brown stirred and sat up. Then the others. The men were a little panicky, but the presence of Brown and Sampson calmed them.

Garth, relieved of guard duty, had fallen asleep almost instantly.

He woke at dawn. Red twilight filtered down from above. The others were lying motionless in their blankets. Sampson's big body was huddled at the base of a tree.

Wearily Garth got up and went over to the giant. "Sampson!" he called. "Wake up! We've got a job—"

He stopped. Sampson's eyes were open, fixed and blank, and his dark cheeks had a significant ruddy flush.

The Noctoli poison—!

Garth stepped back, white to the lips. A sudden, horrible sense of lone-liness pressed down on him. In the jungle things seemed to move, closing in menacingly.

He was alone now.

Alone—with twelve helpless companions to guard!

Somehow—somehow!—he had to get them through. One more day, and they would be at their goal. They could not stay here, that was cer-tain.

Garth searched Sampson's pack till he found a half-empty whiskey bottle. He poured the burning stuff down his throat, though it rocked him back on his heels. But he needed artificial stimulation; it was the only thing that could keep him going now.

It helped. Garth took Sampson's gun and stuck it in his belt. If his own jammed or ran out of ammunition, today, it would be unfortunate.

One more day.

One more day!

Somehow, he got Sampson, Brown and the others lined up. They would march when he gave the word. The hypnotic trance of the Noctoli pollen had turned them into robots.

Garth put Paula directly behind him. The sight of her wan, drawn face made him feel a little frightened, though not for himself. He was remembering Moira, who had died on Earth years ago.

Eleven men and a girl—and he was the only one who could save them.

Garth made sure that the packs were in place on the men's shoulders. He took another drink, pulled out one of the guns, and gave the command to march.

Like automatons the line followed him.

If the day before had been hell, this was double-distilled hell.

Within an hour, Garth's nerves were scraped raw. He had to be constantly alert. The wrenching strain of watching for camouflaged menace made his eyes ache. When movement came, he had to be ready. Ready to squeeze the trigger....

He had to have eyes in the back of his head. For Sampson, at the tail of the procession, was as helpless as the others.

Liquor kept Garth going. Without it, he would have collapsed. By noon he was forced to call a halt, his eyes throbbing with the strain. But even then he could not relax. Danger waited everywhere.

He never remembered what happened that afternoon. He must have acted automatically, through blind instinct. But he got them through, somehow....

It was like awakening from deep sleep. Garth was abruptly conscious that he was marching forward, his head moving rhythmically, his eyes searching the jungle. The red twilight was almost gone.

He whirled, to see Paula directly behind him, unharmed. The others were strung out in single file—all of them, with Sampson's red head at the end. None was missing.

Garth shivered. His body was aching like fire. A quick glance showed him that his clothes were ribboned, his skin scratched raw, a long slash along his ribs. It had been treated with antiseptic, he saw, though he did not remember administering first aid, nor what had caused the wound.

What had wakened him? He peered through the gloom, making out a dark bulk, regular in outline, ahead and to his left. A few paces further gave him the answer. It was a building, of black stone or metal, no more than twelve feet high, and with an archway gaping in the nearest side.

Somehow it struck a chord of memory. They must be near their goal. No savages had built this structure. The Ancient Race?

The Zarno—they might be near by. It would not do to encounter them now, while the men were in their Noctoli trance. And here, in the Forest, they were without cover, at the mercy of the Zarno should they appear.

Garth reconnoitered quietly, leading the others, for he dared not leave them alone. The black building seemed untenanted. He could vaguely make out a flight of steps leading down into darkness, and, more important than that, the threshold itself was thick with dust and mould. The—temple—was empty.

Which made it a good place to hide. Garth was beginning to realize he could not keep going much longer, at least without collapsing. But soon after dark the others would recover from their trance.

He stepped warily across the threshold, into the gloom of the temple. Simultaneously the flooring sank almost imperceptibly beneath his feet, and a deep, brazen bell-note boomed out, hushed with distance, as though it came from underground.

Indecision held Garth motionless for a moment. That clang was a signal of some sort—a warning against trespassers? A warning to *whom*?

* * * *

He was answered quickly. A low cry came, harsh and oddly familiar. It was the first of many. Garth, hesitating on the threshold, uncertain which way the danger lay, instinctively reached out his arm and dragged Paula close. She came obediently to his side, her eyes seeing nothing. The others—they stood like frozen statues.

Something flashed amid the underbrush. The scarlet tangle of vines and leaves was torn aside, and a figure leaped into view.

A figure, man-like—yet not human!

At first glance it seemed to be a man in armor, more than six feet tall, and proportionately broad. Its body gleamed with reflected light. Neckless, its head was a hairless, shining ball whose only features were two oval, jet-black eyes. They were uncannily menacing.

A statue come to life! For the creature's body was obviously not flesh —it was hard, rough and shiny as translucent glass. Silicate life!

Sprung from a silicon chemical base, as Earth life comes from carbon —but sentient, intelligent, and dangerous!

Others like it raced into view, pausing as they saw Garth and his companions. The first stepped forward. He had no mouth, but a circular diaphragm below and between his eyes vibrated rapidly, forming recognizable words.

"*Al-khron ghanro ssel 'ri—*"

It was the Ancient Tongue, which Garth had learned five years before, and never forgotten. It came back to him easily now. He was beginning to remember other things, too. These creatures—he had seen them before. The Zarno—

"We come in peace." He raised one hand, his nerves jolting, waiting for the answer. Presently it came.

"You are not a god. The others with you are not gods. We are the Zarno; we destroy. We guard the house of the gods till they return."

Another of the silicate creatures pushed forward. "Do you not know this being, Kharn? Eight *ystods* ago he came here with another like him. Do you remember?"

Kharn nodded slowly. "That is true. We did not slay them then, for we thought they were messengers from the gods. They pretended to be—we were not sure. This one escaped. The other went into the Darkness."

The other? Doc Willard? Garth felt his throat tighten.

"The—Darkness? What is that?"

"The place from which only the gods return," Kharn said slowly.

Did he mean—death? Before Garth could ask, the second Zarno spoke.

"They must be taken and sacrificed, Kharn."

Garth took out his gun. "Wait," he said sharply, as the Zarno moved forward. "We have weapons. We can destroy you."

"You do not speak the truth. Only the gods can destroy us. Ages ago they came here and built their temple and taught us to be wise. When they left us, we stayed on, to guard the sacred places."

Garth's mouth felt dry. "We *are* messengers from the gods—" he declared.

"It is not true." Kharn began to walk forward. "Take them!"

Garth knew he had lost.

* * * *

It was like a nightmare, the steady, relentless approach of the monstrous beings. Garth held his gun leveled. His arm tightened around Paula's shoulders.

"Keep back," he commanded, conscious of the uselessness of the words.

Instead, Kharn and the others walked on. The creature's shining arm lifted, clamped on Garth's shoulder. He fired.

Kharn did not seem to feel the bullet, though it had not missed. Garth squeezed the trigger again. The pistol jolted against his palm.

The Zarno were—invulnerable!

Garth fought, nevertheless. He could see the silicate men lifting his companions like sacks of meal, hoisting them to gleaming shoulders, and carrying them, unresisting, through the forest. Paula was torn from his grasp. Cursing, he struck out at Kharn's impassive, inhuman face with the revolver-butt. Useless! Nothing could harm these creatures of living stone.

49

Ignoring his struggles, Kharn prisoned Garth's arms and lifted him. Helpless, Garth was carried after the others. He forced himself to relax. A fury of impotent rage flooded him.

He battled it down. Better wait. A chance might come later; just now, there was none. Wait—

Through the forest they went, a score of the silicate creatures, striding like armored giants in the darkening red glow. Not far. A pillar of black metal loomed before them soon, broken by an archway. Two of the monsters guarded it. For a moment Garth mistook the monolith for one of the ebony trees; then he realized his error as they crossed the threshold and began to descend a spiral ramp.

Now there was light, a cool, silvery radiance that seemed to come from the walls. Kharn's footsteps thumped hollow, tirelessly. Sudden weakness made Garth dizzy. He caught a glimpse of a well around which the ramp wound, a pit dropping away to the heart of a world, it seemed.

Utter exhaustion struck him like a physical blow.

CHAPTER VII

He remembered, dimly, what happened after that. It was like a series of fantastic visions, nightmare flashes of memory. At the bottom of the spiral was a cave, reminiscent of Chahnn and the other cities of the Ancients Garth had seen. Enigmatic machines loomed here and there. Unlike Chahnn, this city was lighted with the pale glow that came out of the walls and high-domed ceilings.

Cavern after cavern—peopled with the silicate creatures, filled with the dead machines of the Ancients! And, finally, an immense cave, its floor slanting up to a raised dais at one end. On the platform a throne of black metal stood, and seated upon it was a gigantic four-armed robot, larger than any Garth had ever seen before—standing, it would have been twelve feet tall, he judged.

Garth got only a glimpse of this. He was carried on swiftly to a smaller cavern where metal doors lined the walls. One of these was unlocked. He, with the other Earthmen, was carried within and dumped unceremoniously on the floor. The Zarno departed, clanging the door shut after them.

Then—silence.

Garth staggered to his feet, staring around. The cell was oddly familiar. He had been in it, or one like it, five years ago with Doc Willard. The silvery light came from the wall, and there was a grating in the door. That was all.

He reached the grating and peered out. Two Zarno were on guard not far away. The lock—it might be possible to pick it, Garth thought, but the silicate creatures were invulnerable. So that would do no good.

Captain Brown's clipped voice said, "Where the hell are we, Garth?"

"Huh? Oh, you're awake." Garth laughed harshly. "You should have waked up half an hour ago. Not that it would have done any good—"

Brown stood up stiffly. "What d'you mean? What's happened?"

The others were waking now. For a few moments the cell was a babble of questions. One of the Zarno came briefly to the grill in the door and looked in. Shocked quiet greeted him.

After he had gone, Garth took advantage of the silence to say, "I'll tell you what's been going on, and then I'm going to sleep. I'll go to sleep anyway, unless I talk fast. I'm dead beat."

Sampson squinted at the door. "Tough customers. Shoot, Garth. I've got a hunch we're in a bad spot."

"We are. Listen—" Briefly Garth explained what had happened.

There were questions and counter-questions.

"You can speak their lingo, eh?"

"That won't help, Brown."

"They can't be invulnerable."

"They are—to our weapons. Silicate life!"

"When will they—sacrifice us?" Paula asked, a little shaken, though she tried not to show it.

Garth shrugged. "I don't know. Maybe I can talk 'em out of it. God knows. They worship the gods—the Ancients, I suppose—but they know we're not gods. So that's that."

"Well—"

* * * *

They talked inconclusively. Sampson casually wandered over to the door, found a twisted scrap of wire, and used it on the lock. After a while he called softly to the others.

"This thing's a snap. It won't keep us in here."

Garth came over. "There are guards. It's no use."

One of the Zarno approached and peered in through the grill.

"Kharn has said you will not be hungry long. Tomorrow you will all die. You eat, like the creatures of the forest, do you not?"

"What's he saying?" Sampson muttered.

"Nothing important." Garth switched to the Ancient Tongue. "It will be dangerous to kill us. We are messengers of the gods."

"We will believe that," the Zarno said, "when one of the gods tells us so." He nodded impassively and retreated.

Paula touched Garth's arm. "Isn't there any way—"

"I don't know. Maybe. Maybe not."

"There's light here. There's none in the other cities of the Ancients. That means the power-source still works here. If we can find it—"

Garth couldn't look at her, knowing they were doomed to die the next day. He shrugged, turned away, and found an empty corner. Ignoring the others, he tried to relax on the hard floor. His brain just wasn't working now. It was fagged out. He had a vague hunch that there might be a way out—but he was too exhausted to follow it up now. A few hours' sleep was vital.

But he slept past dawn. When he awoke, he saw the others lying motionless, their eyes fixed in the blank stare of the Noctoli trance.

Glancing at the chronometer on Brown's wrist, Garth figured swiftly. It was past dawn. That meant there was little time left in which to act—provided action was possible. But sleep had refreshed him, though his muscles still ached painfully. He was beginning to remember what his hunch had been.

When he and Doc Willard had been captives, there had been guards only at night. During the long Ganymedean day, none was necessary, for the Noctoli poison had been active then. By day, the Zarno thought, men of flesh were tranced and helpless. Unless—

Garth moved quietly to the door. Through the grill he saw the cave, empty of life. There were no guards. He was glad he had slept past dawn, so that the Zarno were able to believe him entranced like the others.

But what now? Escape? To where? There was still power in the lost city; perhaps the weapons of the Ancients still existed. Weapons stronger than guns to conquer the Zarno! But, regardless of that, it was necessary to find a hiding-place. This was the day of sacrifice.

Ironic thought—a hiding-place in an underground city teeming with the Zarno!

Garth shrugged. The door was locked, he discovered, and it took time to find the twisted wire Sampson had used. Even then, Garth was unable to manipulate the intricate tumblers. He scowled, chewing his lip, and eying the wire. Sampson's skilled fingers were necessary.

He roused the red-haired giant and led him to the door. Sampson looked straight ahead, his eyes dull. He obeyed when Garth spoke—but that was all. Was his skill sufficiently instinctive to be used now?

There was only one way to find out. Garth put the wire in Sampson's hand.

"Unlock the door."

He had to repeat the command twice before Sampson understood. Then the big man bent, fumbling with the lock, working with agonizing slowness.

Hours seemed to drag past before Sampson straightened.

* * * *

Garth tried the door. It opened. The first step was accomplished, anyhow. The others would be more difficult. He was unfamiliar with the underground city. How the devil could he evade the Zarno and find a hiding-place? Alone, he would have a better chance. But he had twelve companions to take with him.

He spoke to each of them. "Follow me. You understand? Follow me till I tell you to stop. Move as quietly as you can."

Then he led them out of the cell.

The city, as he speedily learned, was a labyrinth. Luckily there were innumerable cross-passages. And all the cities of the Ancients had been built along a similar plan. Garth knew the layout of Chahnn, and that helped him now. But there were times when he had to move fast, and the others walked as though striding through water.

"Quick! In here! *Fast!*"

And they would follow him, into a side tunnel, while the heavy, metallic foosteps of the Zarno approached like the drums of doom.

But there was no place to hide permanently. Worst of all, a distant clanging sounded presently, and Garth guessed what that meant. The escape of the captives had been discovered.

Gingerly he skirted the huge cave where the dais was, glimpsing the giant robot in the distance, and shepherding his charges along a twisting corridor that led down. But the footsteps were growing louder. Garth was almost certain that they were following.

He increased his pace, with wary glances behind him. Unless he found a side passage soon, the swift Zarno would speedily overtake them.

"Faster! Move faster!"

The Earthmen tried to obey. Like automatons they ran, their eyes fixed and staring, while the clamor of pursuit grew louder. Looking back, Garth saw a flash of shining movement The Zarno!

"Faster!"

There were no side tunnels. They came out into a small cave, completely empty. It was a cul-de-sac. Light was reflected brightly from three walls.

The fourth wall was dead black—neither rock nor stone. It was like a jet curtain, blocking their path. Garth jerked to a halt, knowing the utter hopelessness of futility. They were trapped now.

The Zarno were pursuing, unmistakably.

Garth took out his useless gun. His face was set in grim lines. What good were bullets against the silicate creatures?

But waiting helplessly was far worse. At least he could try to fight.

He had forgotten to command his charges to halt. Glancing around, Garth saw something that made his eyes widen in incredulous amazement. Paula was walking toward the black curtain—the wall—

She stepped through it and vanished.

Brown followed her. Then another man. And another.

Last of all, Sampson, disappearing like a ghost through the blackness!

Heavy footsteps whirled Garth about. Down the corridor he could see the flashing gleams that heralded the Zarno. His tight grin was a grimace.

"The hell with you, pals," he said softly—and turned again. He raced in pursuit of the others.

Leaped through the dark curtain!

* * * *

54

There was an instant of grinding, jolting shock that left him blind. He staggered, caught himself, and saw that he was in a passage that led toward a distant brightness. Silhouetted against the glow were the moving figures of his companions.

He sprinted after them. But he did not overtake them till they had emerged in a cavern unlike any he had seen before.

"Okay! Stop! Stop, that's right."

They halted, motionless. Garth looked behind him, but there was no trace of the Zarno.

This cavern was lighted like the others. But there were fewer machines. Row after row of the giant four-armed robots stood like an army on the dark-metal floor. The walls were jeweled, thousands of pearly disks studding them. A low humming came from a machine nearby, a tripod with lenses surmounting a square box.

Garth walked through it. He hesitated, glanced around again, and then peered through the lenses.

A voice seemed to speak within his brain.

"—invoked the rule of silence. After that, Genjaro Lo declared that space travel was inevitable and might solve the natural problems of our civilization—"

It had spoken in the Ancient Tongue. And, at the same time, Garth had seen a picture of a huge, four-armed being with a bulging, yet oddly symmetrical head, standing on a rostrum addressing a multitude—

"*Ed!*" The voice rang through the silent cavern. "Ed Garth! You made it!"

Garth whirled. A man had emerged from a cavern-mouth nearby, a short, slight man with white hair and a lined, tired face. He ran forward, his ragged garments flapping, his eyes shining.

Garth said, in a voice like a prayer, "Doc Willard. *You're alive!*"

CHAPTER VIII

Willard gripped his friend's hands. "Alive, yes. If you can call it that. I've been living for only one thing. I knew you'd come back, with help, if you got through. And you did!"

The cavern was spinning around Garth. He braced himself, staring at the man.

"Doc! I've been going crazy for five years. I thought I—I'd killed you."

Willard stared. "Killed me? But—"

"That altar!" The words tumbled out of Garth's mouth. "I couldn't remember much. That damned Noctoli poison—I lost my memory. But I knew I'd tried to knife you while you were stretched out on an altar—"

Sympathy showed in Willard's eyes. "Good Lord, Ed! And you could remember only that? You must have gone through hell."

"I did. I didn't know what—"

"But we planned it. The whole thing. A fake ceremony, to impress the Zarno and give us a chance to escape. They thought we *might* be messengers from their gods—the Ancients—and we told 'em so, after we'd learned their language. The sacrifice—it was a fake, that's all. And it went through as we planned. You pretended to stab me, and while the Zarno were bowing and genuflecting, we got away. At least you did. They recaptured me."

Garth shook his head. "Tell me. I don't know, really."

Willard glanced at the Earthmen, curiosity in his eyes. "You've a bit of explaining to do yourself, Ed. Are they—Noctoli?"

"Yeah. I worked out an antitoxin, but it was stale." Quickly Garth explained what had happened.

"I see. Well—got a cigaret?" Willard sucked the smoke luxuriously into his lungs. "That's good. Five years since I had one of these. Sit down and let's talk. No chairs, but try the floor."

"Okay. What happened to you?"

"Nothing much. When we staged our fake ceremony—the Zarno are plenty religious—I headed for that little black temple in the forest. Know the place?"

"Yeah. That's where they caught us."

"Well, it leads to freedom. There's an underground tunnel that takes you out in a camouflaged hangar. The Ancients had antigravity. I found out later, and their flying-boats were hidden there. They're still good, Ed. They still work. I'd have got away if the Zarno hadn't been right on my heels."

"So?"

Willard nodded. "The controls are easy. A couple of push-buttons and a steering-lever. I'd got a few feet off the ground when a couple of Zarno jumped into the boat with me. They heaved me out and followed. The flying-boat went off to Mars or somewhere, I suppose—it kept on going straight up. But there are others. Only I've never been able to get at them. If I could have, I'd have headed for Oretown, pronto."

Garth's eyes were glowing. "If we could reach that hangar, Doc, we could escape—all of us."

"Sure. Only we can't. Too many guards. It's impossible to get out of this city. I've tried often enough. The only way I managed to survive was by entering the Darkness." His voice trailed away.

"That black wall?"

"It's a vibration-barrier. None of the Zarno can pass it. It shakes them to pieces—destroys them. The Ancients made it, I suppose, to guard their library." Willard extended his hand in a sweeping gesture. "This is it. All the knowledge of the Ancients—tremendous knowledge—compiled here for reference. If we could only get it out to the world!"

Garth remembered something. "Does it mention their power-source?"

"Sure. I've had nothing to do for five years but study the library. I could put my finger on the wire-tape recording that explains the process. It's an intricate business, but we could duplicate it on Earth easily enough."

Paula would be glad to know that, Garth thought. The secret of the Ancients' power, that could replace oil and coal—a vital secret to Earth now.

* * * *

Willard was still talking. "I ran when I heard you coming. I'd been studying one of the recordings, but I thought the Zarno might have got through the barrier somehow.... It doesn't harm humans, luckily, or the robots. I learned a lot in five years."

"How did you manage to keep alive?"

"I found food. The Ancients had stocked up this place. *Pills!*" Willard grimaced. "They kept me alive, and there was a machine for making water out of the air. But I'm hungry for a steak."

Garth scowled. "Doc—one more thing. You know what I mean?"

Willard sobered. "I get it, Ed. The cure. Whether or not I—"

"Whether or not you've found the cure for the Silver Plague. It hasn't been checked yet. It's still killing thousands on Earth."

"So. I wondered a lot about that. Well—the answer is yes, Ed. I know the answer."

"The cure?"

"Yes. I worked it out, completely, with the aid of the Ancients' library. They were studying it too, but they didn't have quite the right angle. However, they were able to supply the missing data I needed." Willard took from his pocket a small notebook. "I had five years to work on it. So far, of course, it's theoretical, but everything checks. It's the cure, all right."

Somehow Garth didn't feel much excitement. Five years ago, he thought, that notebook would have saved Moira's life. Now—well, it would still save life. It would save Earth. But—

He shrugged. "Two good reasons to get back to civilization. The cure, and the secret of the power-source."

Willard nodded. "The Ancients died of the Silver Plague, indirectly. They tried to escape by changing their bodies. The library told me that."

"Their bodies? How?"

"Well—you've seen the robots in Chahnn and here. Originally they were the servants of the Ancients."

"Intelligent?"

"No—not in the way you mean. They could be conditioned to perform certain tasks, but usually they were controlled telepathically by the Ancients, who wore specialized helmet-transmitters for the purpose. The robots had radioatomic brains that reacted to telepathic commands. Then when the Silver Plague struck, the Ancients tried to escape by transplanting, not their physical brains, but their *minds*. I don't quite know how it was done. But the thought-patterns, the individual mental matrix, of each Ancient was somehow impressed on the radioatomic brain of a robot. Their minds were put into the robots' brains—and controlled the metal bodies. So they escaped the Plague. But they died anyway. Human, intelligent minds can't be transplanted successfully into artificial bodies that way. So—in a hundred years—they were dead, all of them."

So that was the secret of the Ancients' disappearance from Ganymede. They had taken new bodies—and those bodies had killed them through their sheer alienage.

Willard crushed out his cigaret-stub. "All the knowledge of the Ancients at my finger-tips, Ed. You can imagine what research I've done!"

"I should have thought you'd have looked for a weapon against the Zarno," Garth said practically. "The Ancients were able to conquer them."

"I did—first of all, after I'd learned how to work the recording-machines. A certain ray will destroy them—a vibrationary beam that shakes them to pieces, disrupts their molecular structure. The only trouble is—" Willard grinned sardonically. "It takes a damn good machine shop to build such a projector."

"Oh. We couldn't—"

"We couldn't. The Ancients left plenty of apparatus here, but not the right kind. Mostly records, and a lot of robots. Sorry, Ed, but unless you brought good weapons with you, you're stuck here with me."

* * * *

Garth looked around to where his companions were standing motionless. "Yeah. Looks like it. Unless we can break through to that hangar of antigravity ships—"

"We can't. The city's full of the Zarno, day and night. And there are always guards outside."

Garth sighed. "The trouble is, unless we get out, nothing can stop the Silver Plague. Not to mention the fuel shortage. Wait a minute. You said the Zarno were superstitious—we tricked them once with a fake ceremony. Couldn't we try that again?"

"I did," Willard told them. "It didn't work. The Zarno know what human beings are like now. Only the gods would impress them—those robots who once were their masters."

Garth stopped breathing for a moment.

"There's a way," he said.

Willard looked at him. "I don't think so. When I saw you'd come back, I hoped for a minute—but it's no use. The Zarno are invulnerable to any weapons we can create here. We can't get out of the city!"

"You said the gods would impress them."

"The gods are dead—the Ancients."

"Suppose one of them came back?"

Willard caught his breath. "What do you mean?"

"Originally the robots were controlled telepathically. Why can't that work now—for us?"

"Don't you imagine I thought of that? But it's no use, without one of them helmet-transmitters. And there aren't any...." Willard sucked in his breath. "Hold on! I'd forgotten something. There's one transmitter left—just one. But it's not a portable."

"Swell!"

"Wait a minute. Come over here." The older man led the way to a tripod-projector, found a cylindrical black object, and slipped it into place. "Look at this."

Peering through the eye-pieces, Garth recognized the great cavern with the dais at one end. The scene shifted, showing the gigantic twelve-foot robot sitting on its throne, a solid block of black metal.

"Watch," Willard said.

A voice spoke in Garth's mind, in the Ancient Tongue. "It was necessary to impress the superstitious Zarno. Thus we created this robot god and placed it on its throne. Its radioatomic brain can be controlled telepathically by means of a transmitter concealed within the throne."

The scene changed, showing the back of the ebony block. A hand, inhuman, six-fingered, came into view—the hand of an Ancient. It touched a concealed spring, and the throne's back slid open, revealing a compartment easily large enough to hold a man.

"Here is the transmitter. It is placed on the head and the will focused on issuing telepathic commands to the robot god on the throne."

There was more, but now Garth watched with only half his mind. He scarcely saw the details of the ritual ceremony with which the Ancients had impressed the Zarno. When the vision vanished, he swung about, a new light in his eyes.

"That's it, Doc! That robot god's going to come to life!"

* * * *

Willard frowned. "*Um-m.* The gadget isn't difficult to operate—I've learned that much from the recordings. You just think hard, that's all. But —"

"The god will come to life and summon the Zarno—all of them. The rest of you can escape while I'm keeping 'em busy."

"Hold on!" the doctor snapped. "Why you? It's my job, if it's anybody's."

"Sorry," Garth said. "It doesn't work out that way. You're the only guy who can cure the Silver Plague. Unless you get out safely, it's the end of Earth."

Willard didn't answer. Garth went on swiftly.

"You could reach the hangar if it weren't for the Zarno. Well, I'll get inside that throne and start the ruckus. That'll give you time." His voice was emotionless.

"How do you know you could reach that temple-cave? The city's full of Zarno."

Garth shrugged. "It's a chance we've got to take. The only one."

Willard chewed his lip. "Why the devil do you have to be the one?"

"Because I know the Ancient Tongue. The robot can talk, can't it? Well! It's between you and me, Doc, and you're the boy who can cure the Silver Plague. You can't get away from that."

"I-I suppose so. But—"

60

"You know the way out. Give me time to reach the temple and begin the ceremony. Then lead the others out. They'll obey you; they're in the Noctoli trance. Get 'em to the hangar and light out for Oretown. Be sure to take the recording of the power-source with you."

"You crazy fool," Willard said through stiff lips. "What about Moira?"

Garth's face went gray. "Moira died years ago," he said carefully. "It was the Silver Plague."

Doc didn't reply. But he nodded as though he had unexpectedly learned the answer to a problem that had been puzzling him.

"Okay," Garth said. "You know what to do. Give me time enough to make it. Then get out of here with the others, fast."

Willard's hand gripped Garth's. "Ed—"

"Forget it."

He moved toward the tunnel-mouth. Paula, he saw, was lying near by, her red-gold hair cascading about her pale, lovely face.

Garth stood looking down at her for a long moment. Then he went on, into the tunnel that waited for him. He did not look back.

Cautiously he stepped through the black curtain, ready to retreat at sight of any Zarno. But the cavern was empty.

If he could make it—!

Noiselessly he stole up the passage. Once he froze against the wall at the sound of distant footsteps. But they faded and were gone.

He came out at last into a corridor he recognized. Far away, he saw the flashing gleam of the Zarno's silicate skins. They were approaching, but apparently had not seen him yet.

He raced for the archway that led into the temple-cavern. If there were any Zarno there, it would be fatal. But luck favored him. The immense room was empty. At the far end the huge robot sat on its jet throne.

Garth sprinted across the floor. He could hear voices growing louder in the distance, and the thumping of the Zarnos' footsteps, but he dared not risk a glance behind. Could he make it?

He jerked to a halt, springing behind the throne, its bulk temporarily hiding him. The Zarno were in the temple-cave now; he could tell that by their voices. Hastily he sought the secret spring.

A panel opened in the ebon block. It was exactly as he had seen it on the tripod-recording machine, a fair-sized cubicle with light coming faintly through a vision-slit in one wall. Garth wedged himself in and slid the panel shut behind him, gasping with relief. Peering through the slit, he found he could see the entire cavern. Three Zarno were approaching.

The robot, seated on the throne above him, was, of course, invisible. Garth stared around, trying to remember the details of the Ancients' recording. A helmet transmitter ... there it was, attached by wires to the low ceiling. Warily Garth slipped it upon his head.

What now?

A flat black plate, like a diaphragm, was set in the wall slightly above his head as he crouched. This hiding-place, he realized, had been built for the larger bodies of the Ancients.

Closing his eyes, he tried to concentrate. Doc Willard had said the helmet-transmitters worked that way. Telepathy—will-power—

"*Stand up!*" he commanded silently to the unseen robot above him. "*Stand up!*"

There was a stir of movement. Garth, peering through the slit, saw the three Zarno jerk to a halt.

One of them cried, "The gods return! *Kra-enlarnov! The gods!*"

* * * *

Garth put his mouth close to the diaphragm. His words, amplified, rolled out through the cavern in the Ancient Tongue.

"Yes—the gods return! Summon the Zarno! Let none fail to obey the summons!"

Shouts went up. The Zarno whirled and raced away. For the moment, Garth was alone.

He concentrated on the transmitter again, commanding the robot to move forward to the edge of the dais, till he could see its back.

"Raise your arm. Step back. Forward again. Back."

It worked. The robot obeyed his mental commands, awkwardly, but— it obeyed.

"Back. Sit on the throne."

A jarring crash deafened Garth momentarily. He had forgotten how huge the robot was. No doubt the creature should lever itself down gradually into its seat, instead of dropping a ton of metal solidly on the black block.

Footsteps again. The Zarno were beginning to pour into the cavern. Huge as it was, they almost filled it. They flung themselves flat, crawling toward the dais, nodding their misshapen heads in awkward rhythm. Their voices were raised in a deep-throated chant.

Garth concentrated. At his mental command, the robot rose and paced slowly forward.

"*Kra-enlar!*"

Garth put his mouth to the diaphragm. His voice crashed out.

"The gods have returned! Hear me, O Zarno!"

"*We hear!*"

"Let no Zarno fail to come to the temple of the gods. Have the guards left their posts?"

"Nay—nay!"

"Summon them," Garth roared. "When the gods speak, all must hearken. Let every Zarno come to me now, or die!"

Some of the creatures raced away and returned with others. The chant continued.

"Have any Zarno failed to heed my summons?"

"None—none! We are here—all!"

Garth nearly shouted with relief. There were almost two thousand Zarno in the cavern, he judged, all genuflecting before the dais. And that meant that the city was unguarded—that Doc Willard could lead the others to the antigravity hangar.

If he could hold the Zarno here!

Garth shook his head, feeling oddly dizzy. He tried to concentrate. At his mental order, the giant robot lifted its arms in symbolic, ritualistic gestures he remembered from the tripod-recorder.

But the dizziness persisted. Garth realized that his lungs were hurting. He found it difficult to draw a deep breath.

Air—he needed fresh air! The inhuman lungs of the Ancients probably were able to endure lack of oxygen far better than the human organism. In any case—Garth realized that the air was getting stale.

He investigated the vision-slit. It was barred by a glassy, transparent pane that seemed as hard as steel. Well, it would be necessary to open the panel behind him—a few inches, anyway. Garth's hand sought for the spring. It was in plain sight; there was no need to conceal it within the throne's compartment.

He pressed it. There was a low grinding that stopped almost immediately. Garth tried again.

Useless. The mechanism, somehow, was jammed. Probably its mechanism had failed when the huge robot had crashed down on the throne.

That meant—

Garth's fingers tried to find some purchase on the smooth surface of the panel. He failed....

A Zarno called a question. Garth turned back to the eye-slit, trying to fight back his dizziness. Heads were lifted, he saw, watching him inquiringly, as though the silicate creatures expected something. Well—

He made the robot move again, its arms reaching out in ancient ceremonial gestures. A gasp of awe came from the Zarno.

Their chant thundered out, deeper, sonorous and inhuman.

* * * *

Garth felt the beginning of a throbbing ache in his temples. He was trapped here. How long could he stand it? He was human, not one of the Ancients. He needed air—

63

He held the Zarno, but not for long. Once more bulbous heads were lifted, oval eyes watching him inquiringly. They were expecting something—what? Garth tried to remember what he had seen in the recorder.

More heads were lifted.

Garth made the robot step forward, raising its metal arms. He had to say something—anything that would hold the Zarno quiet for a while, long enough for Doc and the others to escape. Words he had forgotten since childhood came suddenly unexpectedly to him. The English phrases meant nothing to the Zarno, but the sonorous, powerful chant kept them silent.

"He shall deliver thee from the snare of the hunter; and from the noisome pestilence.... Thou shalt not be afraid for any terror by night; nor for the arrow that flieth by day.... A thousand shall fall beside thee, and ten thousand at thy right hand; but it shall not come nigh thee...."

The agony flamed up again in Garth's brain, consuming, terrible. The huge robot body of the dais swayed, caught itself, and the chant thundered out again through the great cavern.

"If I take the wings of the morning; and remain in the uttermost parts of the sea; even there also shall thy hand lead me...."

The distant, harsh clangor of a bell sounded. Garth had heard it before, when he had crossed the threshold of the black temple in the forest. At the sound the Zarno stirred, and a few of them sprang up.

Garth thrust out his hand, fighting back the pain that tore at him like white flame.

His voice held them—

"The floods are risen, O Lord, the floods have lifted up their voices; the floods lift up their waves.... The waves of the sea are mighty, and rage horribly: but yet the Lord, who dwelleth on high, is mightier—"

He held them. He held them, speaking a tongue they did not know, while his mind shook under the impact of sanity-destroying pain. A slow, sick bitterness crept into his soul. Was this the end—death here, prisoned on an alien world, so far from his home planet?

Death—and for what?

He closed his mind to the thought. Mentally he paced Doc and the others through the tunnel, from the black temple to the hangar. Surely they must have reached it by now! Paula—

That first glimpse he had had of the girl, in Tolomo's drinking-hell—Moira, he had thought then, for an incredible instant. Yes, she had been like Moira. If the paths of destiny had led elsewhere than to the Black Forest of Ganymede, the result might have been far distant. He would not be dying here alone, horribly alone. Moira—Paula—

They were the same, somehow. And Garth knew he had to keep going, till he had saved Paula Trent. A little time—a few moments more, to keep the Zarno in check.

He and Moira had been cheated of their lives, their futures in some way he could not quite understand. But there remained Paula. She must not die. She and the others must get through.

"*Ed.*"

Garth's heart answered that soundless call. His lips formed the name *Moira*.

* * * *

She was there, beside him, and he did not question, did not even wonder. It was enough that she had come back. Her brown ringlets curled about the pale face as he remembered, and the blue eyes held love and—something more.

A message.

"What is it, Moira? What—" He reached out hungry arms.

"Ed. It isn't only us. It's Earth. Don't stop now, Ed. A few more minutes to hold the Zarno back; that will be enough. Be strong. A little time more—such a little time, and then you can rest."

A phantom born of his delirium, Garth knew, but she was no less real for that. He tried to speak and failed. His chest constricted with pain. Outside the altar, the Zarno were stirring uneasily.

"I—I can't—"

"You must."

Anger swept through him. "Why? We've been cheated of everything, Moira! Our heritage—"

She smiled at him, very tenderly. "The grass is still green on the hills of Earth, my lover. Have you forgotten? The little streams that go laughing down the valleys, and the ocean surging up to the white beaches? There are still sunsets on Earth, and men and women will see them for ages to come. Men who might have been our sons; women who might have been our daughters. And they are our children, Ed, as surely as though we had given them birth. For we are giving them life. There will be a future for mankind because of us. We have given up our own lives that our children may live, and go on to glories we can never know ourselves. It is Earth that needs your help now—and that is something greater than either of us."

Something greater....

The Zarno were beginning to move forward, and some of them were sidling toward the passage. Garth, gasping for breath, summoned all his reserve energy. He seemed to feel Moira's cool hand on his shoulder, silently urging him on.

Something greater—

"The days of man are but as grass," he croaked, and the amplified sound went thundering through the temple, halting the Zarno where they stood. They turned again to the altar.

"For he flourisheth as a flower of the field ... for as soon as the wind goeth over, it is gone—"

He held them, somehow, knowing that Moira stood beside him. Toward the end, Garth was no longer conscious of his surroundings. The Zarno swam before his eyes, changing, altering, and abruptly they vanished. In their place was—was—

He saw Earth, as he remembered it, the loveliest planet of all. He saw the heart-breaking beauty of flaming sunsets over the emerald seas, and the snowy purity of high peaks lifting above baking deserts. He felt the cold blast of Earthwinds on his cheeks, the stinging, exciting chill of mountain streams against his skin. There was the warm smell of hay, golden in the fields; the sharpness of eucalyptus and pine; the breath of the little bright flowers that grow only on Earth.

He heard the voices of Earth. The chuckling of brooks, and the deep shouting of the gale; the lowing of cattle, the sound of leaves rustling, and the crash of angry breakers. The soul of Earth spoke to the man who would never see it again.

He listened, while he chanted the majestic, rolling syllables that kept the Zarno in check. Beside him was Moira. Beneath him, his own world, green and beautiful.

And across the emerald planet men and women came marching, sunlight making a golden path for them as they moved out of darkness into the unknown brightness of the future. They were like gods, great-limbed, lovely, and with eyes fearless as a falcon's filled with laughter.

Before their marching feet the road of the ages unrolled. Mighty cities reared to the blue skies of Earth, and ships swept out beyond the stars, binding the galaxies and the universe with unbreakable chains of life. Outward and ever outward the circles of humanity and civilization rippled.

Men and women like gods, unafraid, knowing a life greater than ever before—

And they turned questioning eyes on Garth, asking him the question on which their existence depended.

"Will you save us? Will you give us life? Will you give us the future you yourself can never know?"

Garth answered them in his own way, with Moira beside him. For now it did not matter that he was dying; he had found something greater than he had ever known before.

Through the temple his voice rang like brazen trumpets.

"—the wind bloweth ... and the place thereof shall know it no more...."

* * * *

A panel in the wall by his head lit up, making a square of brightness. He strained his eyes at it, discerning a picture. A scanner of some sort. It showed a transparent ovoid slanting up through the black trees of the forest, a ship with Doc Willard at the controls and eleven men and a girl in the vessel with him—a girl with red-gold hair, going back to Earth, with the knowledge that would save a world from destruction.

He had not failed.

The picture on the scanner darkened. The burning ache in Garth's lungs grew worse. If he could breathe—

On the dais, the robot swayed, its metal legs giving beneath its weight. The crash of its fall brought the Zarno to their feet, frozen with amazement for a moment. Then they moved forward like a wave.

Garth saw them, dimly, through the vision-slit. A white curtain of pain blotted them out. He was dying; he knew that. The shouts of the Zarno came to him faintly,

"the wind bloweth ... and the place thereof shall know it no more...."

But in that place the seeds of the future would grow. Once more Garth saw the children of Earth's unborn generations, and this time the question in their eyes was answered. They would live and go on, to the stars, and beyond.

Moira was beside him. Her cool hand touched his; she came into his arms.

And the white curtain flamed agonizingly for the last time.

Then, mercifully, there was no more pain. Under the black throne Garth's body lay motionless in its strange tomb.

The Zarnos' cries filled the temple as they mourned their dead god— but the man who had saved Earth did not hear them.

www.ingramcontent.com/pod-product-compliance
Lightning Source LLC
Chambersburg PA
CBHW020649130626
46552CB00003B/1459